HANG YOUR HEART ON CHRISTMAS

A HISTORICAL WESTERN CHRISTIAN ROMANCE
(BRIDES OF EVERGREEN BOOK 1)

HEATHER BLANTON

RIVULET PUBLISHING

All rights reserved under International and Pan-American Copyright Conventions. By payment of the required fees, you have been granted the non-exclusive, non-transferable right to access and read the text of this e-book on-screen. No part of this text may be reproduced, transmitted, downloaded, decompiled, reverse engineered, or stored in or introduced into any information storage and retrieval system, in any form or by any means, whether electronic or mechanical, now known or hereinafter invented, without the express written permission of Rivulet Publishing or the author.

This novel is a work of fiction. Names, characters, places, incidents, and dialogues are either the product of the author's imagination or are used fictitiously. Any resemblance to actual events, locales, organizations, or persons, living or dead, is entirely coincidental and beyond the intent of the author.

Cover DESIGN by http://www.roseannawhite.com and Carpe Librum Books

Scripture taken from the HOLY BIBLE,

KING JAMES VERSION - Public Domain

A huge *thank you* to my editors and beta readers: (editors) Kim Huther, Vicki Prather, (readers) Jay Critz, Connie Bartley White, Sue Smith Michaels, Cherie Vanoy Critz, Donna Ball, Kathy Shaffer, and Tonie Collins.

Heather Blanton

Please subscribe to my newsletter
https://www.subscribepage.com/z8i1i3_copy
to receive updates on my new releases and other fun news.
You'll also receive a FREE e-book—
A Lady in Defiance, The Lost Chapters
just for subscribing!

FOREWORD

DEAR READERS,

I would like to again say thank you from the bottom of my heart. I have had such a wonderful time taking you all on some incredible journeys in my books. Along the way, we've become friends. That has been an unexpected blessing. I so truly appreciate your support, your smiles, your comments on my facebook page. I am moved daily by your family photos, your quests to make your dreams come true, the private thoughts you share with me.

I truly value your time and humbly seek to deliver a tale that you will ponder long after you have closed the book or your Kindle. I pray, too, that this story will allow a glimpse of God's perfect love.

It is my sincere hope that this little novella blesses you, prompts you to consider what things are truly important in life, and gives you the courage to lay down the things that suck the life from you. Slow down, give thought to the reason for the season, and fall in love with the One who was born to die for you.

FOREWORD

Merry Christmas
Heather

Beloved, never avenge yourselves,
but leave the way open for God's wrath [and His judicial righteousness]; for it is written
[in Scripture], "Vengeance is Mine, I will repay," says the Lord.
But if your enemy is hungry, feed him;
if he is thirsty, give him a drink; for by doing this
you will heap [a]burning coals on his head."
**Do not be overcome *and* conquered by evil,
but overcome evil with good.**

Romans 12:19-21 Amplified Bible (AMP)

INTRODUCTION

The legendary Elfego Baca is the inspiration behind my hero Robert "Dent" Hernandez.

Elfego's father Francisco was a lawman, and, on occasion, he allowed his son to ride with him in pursuit of some pretty tough hombres. Francisco taught his son to shoot, to ride, to fight, and to wear the badge like a man of justice, not vengeance. He could not have foreseen how well the lessons would stick.

In 1884, nineteen-year-old Elfego learned that the rowdy cowhands from John Slaughter's ranch were running roughshod over the mostly-Spanish community of Lower Frisco, NM. Raping, pillaging, the usual outlaw behavior. Outraged, Elfego somehow wrangled a badge (real, fake, the details are fuzzy) and headed off to clean up the town.

Not long after his arrival, he was alerted to the ungentlemanly behavior of one Charlie McCarty. Drunk and belligerent, McCarty was howling at the moon, firing his gun indiscriminately, and generally scaring the townsfolk silly. Baca arrested the cowhand straightaway.

As is always the case in these situations, things quickly

INTRODUCTION

spiraled out of control and Elfego Baca found himself hiding in a *jacal* (ha-cal – a flimsy structure-like a shack) and being shot at by between *forty and eighty* very annoyed cowboys. Hundreds of thousands of rounds were fired at him during a *thirty-three* hour siege. Just the door to the one room, cedar-and-mud structure was hit nearly four hundred times!

Elfego survived unscathed.

He did, however, kill one cowboy, shoot one horse (which then fell on its rider and killed him), and wound several of his attackers.

When the siege was over, our young lawman still wasn't done. He sent a letter to the cowboys who had tried to kill him. It read, "I have a warrant here for your arrest. Please come in by March 15 and give yourself up. If you don't, I'll know you intend to resist arrest, and I will feel justified in shooting you on sight when I come after you."

Most of the men couldn't surrender fast enough.

Elfego's good fortune and startling bravado was the foundation of his legendary status. He lived a colorful, sometimes controversial, life as a lawman, attorney, politician, and hero. He left behind a statue and some tall tales. I thank him for being the inspiration behind *Hang Your Heart on Christmas*.

This story is dedicated to our own brave lawmen and women and first responders. May I encourage you to never give in, never back down, and never lose faith. We're behind you. Thank you for your courage.

CHAPTER 1

U.S. Marshal Robert "Dent" Hernandez signed the voucher and slid it back across the desk to the sheriff. "That'll do it." *Two down ... how many more to go?*

Sheriff Ben Hayes leaned back in his chair and regarded Dent with that familiar, pitying expression. "Son, aren't you tired?"

Dent held his breath to keep from sighing. Ben, with his barrel-chest and graying hair, was a good man, but he was too eager to share his thirty-years of lawman wisdom. "No, sir." Dent swiped his hat up off the desk. "Bringin' 'em in is my job."

"You know that's not what I'm talkin about. Your pa wouldn't want you throwing your life away on his account."

Dent dropped his hat on his head. "If the men I arrest don't have a chance to kill somebody else's pa, that's not a waste." He touched the brim in good-bye. "I'm gonna go get some lunch. I'll head out with the prisoners after."

He stepped out on the now-sun-washed main street of Evergreen and flinched at the mud. Six straight days of autumn rains had turned the normally dusty street into a quagmire. Off to his left, four men, covered head to toe in the muck, sweated and cursed the mess as they worked to pry their wagon loose. Mules strained and tugged. The sucking sound from the wheels drowned out the noise from the rest of the mud-weary traffic.

"Dent," Ben stepped up beside him, "you don't take a day off. You don't rest. You swing through town once in a blue moon, and then you're gone again. You got roots in this town and they're dying."

"That would be a tragedy."

"You could attend a dance every now and then." Ben wiggled his eyebrows. "Git your arms around a pretty girl. Bid on a sweet apple pie."

Dent didn't care to reply. He continued watching the men mired in the mud. *Most excitement this town has seen in a decade.*

"That hate's gonna eat you up, son. One day you'll wake up fat, old, and alone–like me–and wonder what it was all for."

That last part surprised Dent. "You're a good lawman, Ben. You don't think it's been worth it? Think about who you've helped put in jail."

Ben sighed and swiped his hand over his face. "You're missing my point. You can do your job, and have a life, too. I know that now. I didn't when your pa and I were young."

The fire that burned in Dent's belly didn't agree. One day he would get the final clue. One day he would arrest the men who had shot his father. He could wait. He could be patient. He could not, however, waste time attending dances and sampling pies. "I thank you for your advice, Ben. You know I respect your opinion."

Ben laid a hand on Dent's shoulder, a breeze stirring his faded brown hair. "Say the word, and you can be my deputy any time."

He bit back a derisive snort. Evergreen, a nice, quiet town, was just the place for a middle-aged lawman tired of chasing criminals. Nearing thirty, Dent was *not* middle-aged or tired. "Well, I thank you for the offer. And I will consider it."

"Yeah, sure you will." Ben squeezed his shoulder and went back inside.

At the depot, Dent tugged at the shackles on his prisoners, hands then feet, then stepped back to stand beside Ben. The two lawmen appraised the offenders. "Happy" Jack Briscomb—short, stocky, face bruised from tripping over Dent's fist—scowled like he was anything *but* happy. His comrade, Needles Jones, a slender, dark-haired fella with one wayward eye, glared at them as he defiantly clanked the shackles at his wrists.

Ben tagged Dent in the ribs. "Watch him," he motioned to Needles. "He's got a bad temper ... Why he's in trouble in the first place."

"Will do." Dent walked around behind the men and gave them a nudge. "All right, boys, here comes the train." The two shuffled over to the edge of the platform. The deafening chug-chug-chug drowned out any further conversation as they waited for the crawling iron horse to enter the station. Amidst the hiss and steam and an ear-splitting whistle, the *Cheyenne to Lander* slowed and halted.

The conductor jumped down and set the step in place for the passengers. One by one, dusty cowboys, slick salesmen in cheap suits, and harried mothers battling defiant toddlers, emerged from the train. Some embraced their loved ones. Others disappeared into the swirl of bodies. Dent's gaze darted all around, looking for trouble, intent on preventing his charges from getting any stupid ideas. Trouble could always come anytime, anywhere, from fellas like these. He doubted whether the folks of Evergreen could take the shock.

When a lull in the debarking hit, he shook Hayes's hand. "I'll try to stay longer my next time through."

"I'll hold you to it."

Dent pushed his prisoners forward, but had to wait again as a green cotton dress flitted down the steps. "Pardon us, ma'am," he said, pulling Happy and Needles back by their collars.

He couldn't help but notice the dress was filled nicely with a pretty, young gal, wearing silver-rimmed glasses. Thick, wavy, auburn hair, held partially in a barrette, hung at her shoulders, wispy curls framed a sweet, but intelligent, face.

Her eyes, a sparkling, mesmerizing blue, passed over the men then suddenly widened with stark terror. In a blur of motion, Needles reached back and clawed for Dent's gun. Dent felt the revolver slipping from his holster, and grabbed for it. His grip was awkward at best, obstructed by his prisoner's chains and handcuffs.

Needles jerked the gun free, spun, and fired. The young lady and the women nearby screamed, men gasped. Folks scrambled for cover. Somehow, the shot missed Dent, and Needles, reacting as fast as a riled snake, draped his shackled arms over the terrified woman. Dent moved to lunge. The outlaw clutched the woman tighter and stepped back with her, shaking his head. He raised the revolver and cocked the hammer.

Dent clenched his jaw and stilled.

The young lady paled to the pallor of chalk dust, and appeared to quit breathing.

"You ain't hanging me, lawdog." Needles splayed one hand

over the girl's midsection. His filthy fingers caressed her ribs. "Now git me a horse or I'm gonna drop her."

A deep, black, slithering hate rose up in Dent as he evaluated the outlaw. A greasy creature, he was just the sort who would shoot a woman. He was here now because he'd snapped and shot a blacksmith in Topeka. Unpredictable with that temper of his.

"Hey, hey, hey." Happy threw his shackled hands in the air and took two steps away from the fracas. "I don't want no part of this, Marshal. I ain't in on it." He swiveled to Needles. "You don't know what you've done. You don't know who he is."

Grinning, Needles pushed the barrel of the gun into the cleft between the woman's breasts, eliciting a whimper from her. "Ask me if I care. Git me a horse, Marshal. I'll leave the lady and ride out. No harm done."

The woman's eyes spoke volumes. *Save me, please,* she implored silently. He noted absently that her peril should affect him. But all he cared about was how the next few seconds were going to play out.

He flicked his wrist, and the Derringer slid into his hand. His arm shot out like a lightning bolt and he squeezed the trigger. Needle's head jerked with the report of the gun. Blood and brain matter exploded out the back of his head. The lady screamed, her eyes rolled back in her head, and both she and the outlaw hit the ground.

"Dent," Ben's labored, breathless voice came from behind.

Keeping his gun pointed at Needles, Dent glanced back, then looked again. Blood gushed from Ben's chest. His gaze bored into Dent as he reached out. "Sorry, son ... I wish I'd ..." Ben's knees buckled.

Dent rushed to him, heedless of Needles or the woman. "No, Ben," he caught his friend as he pitched forward. *No, not Ben ...*

CHAPTER 2

*D*ent wouldn't have thought it possible that such a catastrophe could unfold in Evergreen, of all places. If only he hadn't been distracted, for the breath of an instant, by shimmering, blue eyes.

Sick over his costly stupidity, he pinched the bridge of his nose and dropped down into a chair at Doc Woodruff's office. Somehow, in one terrible, swift moment, he'd shot his prisoner dead, scared an innocent by-stander out of her wits … and lost the man who had been a second father to him.

The shot still rang in his ears

He touched the blood-soaked bib of his shirt, incredulous.

Ben was dead.

At least, so was Needles. Good riddance.

Dent struggled with the way his grief gave way too easily to the thirst for revenge. He couldn't arrest 'em all, but he had made another permanent dent in the criminal population. He laughed inwardly at the reminder of the nickname. Courtesy of Ben Hayes, now deceased.

Doc Woodruff sat down in the chair across from Dent, removed his glasses, and rubbed his eyes. "I'm sorry. Ben was a good man. I can hardly believe he's gone." He slipped the glasses back on then scratched the silvery beard at his jaw. "The whole town will miss him, but his death sure leaves us with a problem. We've got no law here now. Word gets out—"

"Can't help ya. I've still got a prisoner to deliver to Cheyenne."

"Lock him up and wire for another deputy to do it."

Dent chafed at the suggestion. He always finished the job. But he had surely made a mess of this one. How in the heck had Needles grabbed his gun? One pretty face ... one instant of distraction ... then eternity for Ben; which made finishing this job all the more vital. "You know I can't do that."

Doc pursed his lips, as if the objection proved a point. "Dent, maybe it isn't my place to say this, but you're not exactly winning any prizes for the way you handle your duties. Sometimes, it's a nice surprise to hear you've delivered prisoners who are still upright in the saddle, 'stead of slung across it."

"I never shot or killed anybody that wasn't tryin' to kill me. I don't start trouble, but I finish it."

Doc frowned at him, raising an eyebrow in a that's-not-the-whole-truth-and-you-know-it look. "I'm just saying maybe you could stand to relax a bit. I treated veterans after the war like you—the ones who had seen a lot of fighting. You're too ready to kill, Dent. Specializing in dying is no way to live."

Dent readied all kinds of justifications for what he did, but Ben's words came back to him. *One day you'll wake up fat, old, and alone—like me—and wonder what it was all for.*

"Anyway, my point is," Doc continued, "taking over for

Ben for a while might show the folks in Evergreen and elsewhere you're not such a hothead. That you can cool down and back off when need be. And I think it would be good for *you* to quit hunting men for a while."

To Dent, staying in Evergreen for any reason sounded like a punishment akin to working a chain gang. Only a chain gang would be more exciting. He did owe Ben something, though, and most likely, there were some pretty ruffled feathers after this fiasco. His negligence had cost the town a good man and a fine sheriff. Dent didn't have a clue how he was ever gonna get past that, but sitting around watching mud dry didn't sound like the way to do it.

Doc slapped his knees and stood, Dent with him. "You think on that. And, while you're thinkin', you might want to pop your head inside my examination room and apologize to the lady whose head you fired at."

"I didn't fire at *her* head."

"She doesn't know that. For all she knows, you could've missed Needles." He tossed up a hand. "I know, I know, you don't miss. But it would be a nice gesture on your part to apologize to the girl. Heck of a welcome for our new schoolteacher. I'm not sure she'll stay now. She's pretty rattled by the reception." Doc winced at Dent's shirt. "And all that blood isn't gonna help. Why don't you change first? I've got a spare I'll loan you."

Dent sighed, a deep, weary exhalation of grief and frustration. "Sure."

---

*A*lone, sitting on the bed in the examination room, Amy stared at her hands. Would they ever quit shaking? Echoes of the gunfire resounded in her head. She plastered her palms over her ears in a futile effort to stop the noise.

She could still feel that vile man holding his hand against her stomach, his hot, sweaty body pressed to hers, and the cold point of the gun barrel between her breasts.

Somehow, it all blurred together with the attack back in Swanton. The acid taste of fear in her mouth, the men grabbing at her and spinning her around, the sound of her dress tearing, and the stench of cheap whiskey and filth filling her nostrils.

Her hand crept around to the back of her head as she recalled the pain of her skull smacking the sidewalk. It all still felt so real, as real as if she was back there again, screaming, clawing, the cold air swarming her shoulder as her dress was ripped away, that chilling laughter ... and the single pistol shot that chased the attackers away.

She covered her face with her trembling, fragile hands, and stifled the sobs crying for freedom. Slow, determined tears spilled down her cheeks. *Oh, God, why has all this happened? I feel like a shell of who I was. I'm so afraid ...*

"Uh, ma'am?" a male voice called through the door as he knocked gently.

Amy wiped her face and squared her shoulders, but she didn't have the energy to stand. "Yes? Come in."

A handsome young man with shoulder-length, wavy, black hair and eyes the color of chocolate drops peered around the door; the marshal who had shot at her ... or, rather, at her *assailant*. His square, handsome face, full of trepidation, warmed a bit and he nodded as he stepped into the room. "I'm U.S. Marshal Robert Hernandez. I wanted ..." he trailed off and shrugged. "Um, I guess, to apologize. I'm sorry for all this trouble. I hope you're all right."

Amy stared at him, clueless as to a response. She didn't feel all right, not at all. "You could have shot me," slipped out.

It felt good to let a little of the fear mix with some anger, and she rose. "What if you'd missed? Did you really think the place for a shoot-out was a crowded train platform? What kind of town is this?" Hysteria tried creeping into her voice. "I came here because I was assured Evergreen was a safe, quiet community with virtually no crime and, yet, I'm thrust in the middle of gun-play before I even step off the train."

"Ma'am," Dent patted the air and spoke gently. "I am truly sorry for what transpired. I'm truly sorry you were caught in the middle. However, I can assure you what happened today probably won't happen again in Evergreen for another hundred years."

Amy sank suddenly to the bed, her knees going all weak and wobbly. Peace and quiet. Crickets. Law-abiding residents. More churches than saloons. Her physician had assured her Evergreen was the perfect place to quiet her fears and calm her nerves. She closed her eyes and tried slowing her racing heart. She despised this feeling of being so ... emotionally precarious. "I was told there was no crime here. Not even petty larceny. Is that true, Deputy Hernandez?" She lifted her gaze to him, and was surprised to find him staring back with a mixture of concern and confusion.

"I give you my word, Miss, Evergreen is one of the finest, safest towns in the West. You couldn't be any safer if you were back East."

She bit back a bitter laugh. "The East certainly isn't what it used to be ... but I thank you for your assurance." She scanned the spartan little room and realized none of her belongings had come with her. Attempting to pull herself together, she stood once more and faced the marshal. "My things. My suitcases, satchel—"

Marshal Hernandez opened the door all the way and motioned to the outer room. "I'm sure between Doc and me, we can find your items and get you settled ... um, wherever you'll be staying." Amy nodded a quick thank-you and moved to exit the room. As she passed by the marshal, he leaned in a little. "And one other thing, Miss."

She paused, waiting.

"I wouldn't have shot you by accident. I never miss."

CHAPTER 3

"I'll take care of the bags, dear." Doc closed his office door behind the plump Mrs. Woodruff and the much more petite Miss Tate. Through the window, Dent absently watched the ladies amble down the boardwalk. His mind was back at the jail wondering when he could head out with Happy.

Grinning, Doc tagged Dent in the ribs. "Yep, I guess I'd stare, too, if I was a young, single man."

Dent didn't catch Doc's drift at first, but then he shook his head. "No sorry. I was lookin' in her direction, but thinking about Happy Jack. I need to go check on him and get my report written."

Doc reached up and laid the back of his hand on Dent's forehead, then touched the pulse at his neck. Flustered, Dent swatted his hand away. "What's the matter with you? I ain't sick."

Doc dropped his hand onto his hip. "I'm trying to make sure you're not *dead*. You even notice how pretty that gal is?"

Dent let his gaze drift out the window again. "Maybe."

Which was the same thing as saying *not really*. "I've had a few things on my mind in the last hour."

"True." Doc sighed at the reminder of Ben's death, tugged his hat from a hook, and grabbed the doorknob. "Well, she's my houseguest till her cabin's ready. You come by for dinner. Maybe you'll take a minute to notice." He pulled the door open.

"I noticed her on the train, and now Ben's dead."

Doc stopped in his tracks. He thought for a moment then wheeled around to Dent. Sixty or so, he was still tall and straight, and carried himself with authority. "It's not that girl's fault."

Dent flinched at the steel in his friend's tone. "No sir. I didn't mean to imply it was."

The apology seemed to satisfy Doc. He nodded and slipped through the door. Dent was a little surprised by the man's unusual *protectiveness* of the new schoolteacher, but didn't give it much heed. His own misery and guilt crowded out the observation as he dropped his hat onto his head.

"A deal? You want to make a deal?" Dent looked past a wide-eyed, hopeful Happy Jack, to the bars in the cell's window. He thought about all the times he'd passed through Evergreen on his way to find some outlaws. Ben had been a solid reminder that good men, law-abiding men, still held sway in the country. Now, he was gone and Dent had a good mad on. He was as surly as a bear. "No, Jack, I ain't too interested in a deal."

"Aw, come on, Marshal." Jack approached the bars. "I didn't know what Needles was gonna do and I didn't help him. I stepped outta the way. That oughta be worth somethin'."

"Not really."

Jack scowled at Dent's deadpan answer. Then an evil tease lifted his brow. "What if I had some information?"

Dent sniffed and rested his hand on his gun. "For instance?"

The criminal grinned, showing a mouth full of rotten or missing teeth, and clutched the bars. "I hear tell every time you arrest somebody, you ask 'em a question."

"Which is?"

"Somethin' about 'was you in Sheridan on July 10, '67?'"

"Were you in *Evergreen*, on or about the evening of July 3, 1880?"

"Yea, that's it." Jack squinted. "Why that date?"

"You said somethin' about some information."

Jack hesitated for a moment. "What if it *is* worth somethin' to ya?"

"I might mention to the territorial judge how you were not involved in the fray at the depot, and that you did not aid Needles in his attempt to escape ... but I wouldn't bet on it."

Jack thought about it long and hard then shrugged, as if he didn't have anything to lose. "I was in Fort Carson a few months ago. Played poker with a fella that said he shot a Wyoming lawman and probably would never step foot in the territory again. The lawman had a son who wouldn't let it go."

Dent had to admit the piece of information was intriguing, though specifics would have been helpful. When and where in Wyoming had this supposed murder taken place? On its own, another useless clue. But the part about the lawman's son piqued his interest. "He didn't say a name? His or the lawman's? Can you describe this fella?"

"I did not get his name, or any others, but he wore a stovepipe hat and had bad scars on his wrists, like he'd been—"

"Shackled? Like he'd been on a chain gang?"

Jack smiled, big and wide. "Now that's information you can use."

Possibly. Identifying marks were usually mentioned on Wanted posters and the scarred wrists could mean the man had been on a railroad chain gang. "Fort Carson, huh?" Yes, these were solid leads. "I'll be sure the judge knows what happened today, Jack."

CHAPTER 4

Ben had saved all the Wanted posters that came into his office. He had a collection going back twenty years. Dent pulled open the top drawer of the filing cabinet and scooped up an armful. If it took till the Second Coming, he would go through every one of these.

The second step he'd take care of on the way to Doc's house. He'd send a telegram to the Union Pacific asking for the names of the prisons that had supplied chain gangs between the peak building years of '65 to '70. A shot in the dark, but maybe he'd get lucky and match some names with these Wanted posters.

He dropped into the squeaking, leather office chair at the desk ... and froze. How many times had Ben settled his old bones into this very seat and recalled his days chasing outlaws with Pa? Dent had loved those stories about the wild-and-wooly pair of lawmen.

Now both of them were gone.

And Dent felt ... lost.

He rubbed his temples and tried to think about business. The report he'd have to write ... explaining how he'd let a killer get hold of his gun. Most likely, the report would end his career, and maybe that was as it should be. Penance.

Sagging inside, he leaned back in the chair and stared at the ceiling. *No way to fix this mess.*

Then plow right through it.

Working was better than wallowing in self-pity and grief. Determined not to waste a potential lead, he started flipping through the posters. The report, though, haunted his mind, poked at him like a kid with a stick. He couldn't sugarcoat a dang thing. Nothing he could do, in fact, except spell it out.

He shook his head and stood. If he had to write the report that would end his career, he could at least do it with a good dinner in him. He wouldn't shirk it. He'd write it tonight while it was still fresh in his mind then turn it in tomorrow when he delivered Happy ...

And let the chips fall where they may.

"Dent, I hate to talk about this at dinner," Doc ladled steaming chicken and dumplings onto his plate, the aroma filling the small dining room. "And I especially hate to talk about this in front of Miss Tate," he nodded at the schoolmarm, "but, well, you're the only thing Ben's got for family. Least ways no one's seen his wife and son in years." He returned the spoon to the pot and settled back. "We need to make arrangements, and I know for a fact he left you his ranch—"

"His ranch?" Dent nearly choked on a dumpling. "He left me his ranch?"

"Oh, I know it doesn't really qualify as a ranch, what without cattle and all, but it's a fine spread. You could fix it up and—"

"No, no, no," Dent waved his hand, earning him a

confused, almost fearful, look from Miss Tate. "I can't be tied down to property."

Dent's emphatic reaction brought the table to a halt. Susan Woodruff frowned hard and clutched the schoolteacher's hand, as if to assure her the U.S. Marshal wasn't coming unglued. "Dent, no need to get so excited," she said gently. "If you don't want the property, you can always sell it, like you did your pa's place. The more immediate need would be to talk to Pastor Wills to arrange Ben's funeral."

Dent sighed so heavily he 'bout blew the food off the table. He wasn't prepared for any of this. Dang, he wished he could shoot Needles again, just to make himself feel better. "Susan, I'm between a rock and a hard place." He rubbed his jaw and shifted his attention to Doc. "I've got that business tomorrow over in Cheyenne."

Doc's eyes narrowed and he and Susan swapped strained glances. Unspoken messages swirled at the table. Perhaps aware there was something here that was none of her business, Miss Tate dropped her head as if her vittles had suddenly become more interesting.

"Yes, that business," Doc repeated. "Not something you can get out of, at least not at this late date."

"Henry and I can talk to Pastor," Susan offered. "We'll make the arrangements, if that's all right with you."

"That's best, Susan, if you don't mind. Thank you." And Dent truly was appreciative. The feeling he was drowning rose up in him. Given the choice, he preferred a hanging to making funeral arrangements and wondered what that said about the condition of his heart.

Specializing in dyin'...

"Miss Tate," Susan shifted her attention to their guest, "this *can* wait until after supper," she flicked a warning glance at Doc. "Let's talk about something more pleasant. You." She patted the girl's hand. "I understand you were a librarian most recently, but you have been a schoolteacher?"

Dismissed from the conversation, and glad of it, Dent hunkered down over his food and focused on eating.

"Yes ma'am." The girl laid her fork down and shoved her glasses up a bit. "I taught elementary school for six years, but I love books so much that when I had the opportunity to move to the library, I jumped at it."

Dent stabbed a dumpling and almost laughed at the girl's history. Since she was about as exciting as a brick, he figured she'd fit right in with Evergreen. A schoolmarm *and* a librarian. At least he'd never be arresting her for anything. And maybe he *had* noticed she was a little on the pretty side. He risked a quick glance to confirm that. Her cheeks were soft and smooth, flawless, and the color of a ripe peach. Dainty auburn curls wafted gently around her face as she moved. Dent ducked back to the safety of his meal.

Doc pushed a biscuit around his plate as he sopped up the remaining chicken broth. "In case you were wondering, Miss Tate, the town doesn't know much about your personal history."

An odd, stilted tone in the man's voice drew Dent back in. He saw the cautious exchange between Miss Tate and her hosts. Something had been said without being said, but he couldn't have cared less. He had his own matters to worry about.

Susan picked up the pitcher and poured more water for herself and Miss Tate. "The search committee tells me you will be starting a library as well as teaching?" Dent heard the forced cheer, getting them past the unspoken message.

"Yes ma'am." Miss Tate wiped her mouth and set her napkin on the table. "Because of my work at the library, I've met many, many patrons who love to share the joy of reading. I'm sure we'll have hundreds of books donated by spring."

"Oh, that's so exciting. I love to read, too." Susan rose and started to clear the table. "Well, we'll have dessert and coffee in the living room."

"Let me help," Miss Tate started to rise.

"No, no," Susan shook her head. "You're a guest. You and Dent go on in." She waved a hand toward the hallway. "Henry and I will bring in the pie." Susan pulled Dent's plate away from him, although he wasn't done. He followed it stubbornly for a moment, but her raised brow convinced him to let it go. Not sure why she was in such a hurry to get him away from the table, he licked his fork, and surrendered it. "Fine. I'll stoke the fire." He rose and left the room.

---

*A*my could have huffed her indignation at the marshal's abrupt departure from the room, but clearly he would not have noticed. He seemed *totally* absorbed in his own matters.

"He was raised better, Miss Tate," Doctor Woodruff rose and proceeded to assist his wife by picking up his own plate and glass. "I hope you'll overlook his preoccupation. It's been a difficult day for him ... for everyone."

"Ben was probably his oldest friend." Susan hoisted a stack of dirty dishes to her hip and hooked two mugs with her fingers. "And ... he's never dealt well with grief."

Considering the circumstances, Amy should have let it go. Not being escorted from the dinner table by a gentleman was certainly not the worst thing that had ever happened to her. No, it was more than that. The marshal looked right through her, as if she wasn't even in the room. She'd been through quite a bit lately, but still had some pride. Being treated as if she were no more important than a rug on the floor stung.

Susan backed up to the kitchen door, her arms full of dishes. "Go on, now. We'll be right there with the pie and coffee."

Amy nodded at her and Doc and slipped across the hallway to the parlor. She found the marshal kneeling at the fire, his hand resting on the poker, his thoughts somewhere far away. She hesitated interrupting his reverie and took the moment to study him. Obviously not yet thirty, weathered lines fringed the corners of his eyes, giving him an air of wisdom and experience men back East didn't possess. His brooding reminded her of Emily Bronte's Heathcliff. She would admit, though, there was something *comforting* about him. She attributed this feeling to his badge.

That night intruded on her thoughts again, threatened to start her heart racing, and she knew it would be a long, long time before she ever let a man near her again ... even a lawman. She pushed the hopelessness of the future away and laced her fingers over her stomach, quelling the queasy feeling trying to rise in her. After a moment, he still hadn't noticed her standing there. A little frustrated, she stepped quietly into the room, allowing the swish of her skirt to announce her. He rose to greet her ... and said absolutely nothing.

The awkward moment stretching on to ridiculous lengths, Amy finally thought of something to rescue them. "I'm sorry for your loss. I understand the sheriff was a friend."

"Yes ma'am. Thank you."

The silence fell again. The marshal shoved his hands into his pockets and smiled weakly. She had seen men who were socially inept and men who were disinterested in conversation. Amy realized he gave *disinterested* new meaning.

Breaking eye contact as a mercy to him, she dipped her head, smiled, and strode over to the settee. Taking a seat, she sighed inwardly. As a houseguest, she certainly couldn't pick and choose the Woodruffs' company. And she supposed she should be grateful the marshal wasn't a chatting magpie.

But neither was he pleasant. Oh, she knew she should make allowances for his circumstances, but his brusqueness was annoying. And frankly, rude. She hoped to avoid him as much as possible in the future.

CHAPTER 5

*H*ands clawed at Amy in the cloistering blackness, trying to strangle her. Screams—hers—interwove with deep, ominous laughter. The sounds echoed all around her. She fought, struggled, writhed, trying to get away. Fear burned in her blood. Her heart raced, pounding hard like a drum in her ears. The hands reached her throat. She opened her mouth to scream—

And sat bolt upright in a strange bed, her fingers pressed against her lips. Breathing hard like a winded horse, she took in the room, unfamiliar and menacing in the moonlight. An open wardrobe loomed like a bear. A dress form stood in the corner like a watchful ghost. She hid her face in her hands and tried to rein in her galloping pulse. She breathed. She prayed for peace. She listened to the silence.

The panic retreated and she slowly climbed from the bed. Rubbing her arms against a non-existent chill, she trudged to the window. From the second floor of the Woodruffs' home, which sat on a hill, she had a high, wide view of Evergreen. Awash in the silvery radiance of a full moon, the town slumbered peacefully. Somewhere off in the distance, a coyote yipped and howled as bats dove and twirled in the night. Amy leaned her forehead against the chilly glass and wondered when she might, finally, sleep without nightmares.

Movement below drew her attention to a shadowy figure. A man stepped out from beneath the eaves of the bank, scanned the street, hunched over, and hurried down the side of the building. At the corner, he knelt down and ... reached beneath the bank, as if stashing something ... or retrieving something. Amy couldn't tell in the darkness. Either way, he quickly got to his feet and ran off behind the building.

She watched for a few more minutes, but the man did not return.

A yawn reminded her that the bed was growing cold, and sleep beckoned enticingly. With a last glance back at the bank, Amy crawled beneath the covers and curled into a warm, cozy little ball. In the morning, she would tell someone what she'd seen.

---

*A*my arrived at the one-room schoolhouse a good thirty minutes before her students were due. She walked in the front door and discovered, to her delight, three young girls in pinafores, dusting her desk, arranging flowers in a pail in the center of it, and washing the chalkboard. They appeared to range in age from about eight to fifteen or so, and had to be sisters. All three had blonde hair, stout builds, and round faces.

They stilled in their activities when they saw her, then huge grins split their faces and they rushed toward their new teacher, all speaking at once.

"It's our new teacher!"

"You're so pretty!"

"Do you like the flowers?"

Laughter, rich and sincere, bubbled up from deep within her, and she let it gush out. She had hardly smiled in the last several weeks, much less laughed, and knew in an instant that God had sent her to the right place. She hugged the little girls and then took a step back from them. "Thank you so very much for this wonderful welcome, girls." She reached for the oldest one's hand. "I'm Amy Tate."

The girl, fresh-faced, with rosy cheeks and a big smile, was built like a lumberjack. She shook Amy's hand, squeezing it firmly and with eagerness. "Yah, it is good to meet you, too. I am Lisette." Her German accent was quite pronounced, but Amy got the gist. "These are my sisters, Greta ... and Matilda." Each youngster curtsied as her name was mentioned.

"I am nine," Greta announced with pride.

"And I am twelve," Matilda curtsied again.

The girls were simply precious, and Amy was delighted with her new friends. She prayed the rest of the class would be so welcoming.

Dent settled into the cowhide chair in front of Judge Lynch's desk and leaned toward his boss. "You wanted to see me, sir?"

The judge looked up from the report he was reading—Dent's report—and the hard steel in his eyes hinted at a storm. Lynch was old, rumored to be eighty, but still sharp, with a mind that used a black-and-white approach to legal affairs, and moved faster than a locomotive. Dent suspected he was about to be hit by that train.

"First things first. How was the hanging?"

"Clean, sir."

Judge Lynch leaned back in his chair and laced his fingers

over his sizable gut, regarding Dent with a displeased expression. "Then let's cut to heart of this, son. On top of complaints in the last two years from two sheriffs and one marshal about your heavy-handed tactics, now I've got this report in which you confess to negligence. Negligence that cost the life of a prisoner and one fine man who was an outstanding law enforcement officer."

Dent licked his lips. He didn't know any formal complaints had been filed. Ben's death on top of those didn't bode well. "I'm willing to take full responsibility, sir."

"Darn right you will." The judge took a deep breath, as if to keep his temper from flaring out of control. Seemingly satisfied, he leaned forward and picked up the report. "Dent, you're one of the bravest officers I have, and I'm fully aware you do what you do because you're hunting for your father's killer, but lately you've become ... well, I don't think it would be a stretch to call you an avenging angel. In fact, I've heard you referred to as the Grim Reaper." Dent started to protest, but Judge Lynch tossed up a finger, cutting him off. "Vengeance and justice are not the same things. I feel you've gotten the two confused. Or maybe you never had 'em right in the first place."

"Beg your pardon, Judge, but does it matter? I have arrest warrants in my pocket when I go after these men. When they resist arrest, I'm within my rights to do what needs to be done. Why do my motivations matter to the law?"

"They don't. They matter to me. "

The clipped answer surprised Dent, and he didn't understand it. The judge must have read his confusion. Wagging his head, the big man rose slowly and wandered over to a bust of Abe Lincoln. "Dent, you're a good man, but you don't see the whole puzzle ... just your piece of it. I thought when I let you on the force—which I did because your father and Ben always spoke so highly of you—I thought you would come to understand the difference between peace officer and vigilante. When you go after a man and your motivation is vengeance, what makes you different from him?" He raised an elbow and rested it on Abe. "You need some time to think things through. I only wish I'd done this sooner."

"Done what?"

"You're hereby suspended, pending an investigation into Sheriff Ben Hayes's death. Suspended without pay."

Dent jumped to his feet. "Without pay?"

Lynch straightened up, daring Dent to challenge him. "And, per a request from a fine, upstanding member of the community, you will—in the meantime—act as the interim sheriff in Evergreen."

Dent's knees almost went out from underneath him.

"Oh," Lynch returned to his desk and sat down, "your other duties will not be impacted by this suspension. You have a gift, and we need it."

CHAPTER 6

Dent kept a few things at a boarding house in Cheyenne and his horse down at the livery. Mad enough to spit nails, he collected everything and saddled Ginger, cursing Judge Lynch underneath his breath as he tossed his saddlebags over the horse's rump. Checking the cinch one last time, he stepped up into the saddle ... and sat there.

Evergreen.

He hadn't spent more than a night or two there since his pa was killed. Nothin' but bad memories haunted the place.

Well, he hoped everybody was happy. Doc musta written the request out for him to be sheriff in town. He reckoned he'd be eternally grateful and would make sure Doc knew *how* grateful.

Since he owned it now, Dent would stay at Ben's ranch ... which felt all wrong. It wasn't Dent's place. Never could be.

At least money wouldn't be an issue. Dent made a good living from his gift, as the judge had called it. In between engagements, however, he figured he would go stark-stirring, ever-loving nuts in *quaint* Evergreen. What was there to do if he could not get his warrants and go after the bad men that needed hanging?

Fit to be tied with this turn of events, he spurred Ginger and headed off for his personal purgatory.

---

*A*my stood behind her desk, smiling and waving as her students filtered out into the late afternoon sunshine. Overall, she counted the day a success. She was relieved and exhausted, but, best of all, *excited*. She liked her students, and they seemed to like her. For the first time in a long time, she had hope the future was still bright.

The room emptied, and she realized one student still remained at his desk. Israel Packett had snuck in late, sat in the back, and didn't say much the whole day. At recess, he and the older boys had played baseball together. A lanky teenager of fourteen or fifteen, with disheveled chestnut hair, and scrawny arms that poked too far out of his sleeves, he reminded Amy of her little brother George.

Like George, Israel was a bit quiet. She sensed the boy was liked well enough, as it had been a friendly, boisterous baseball game earlier in the day. Yet, when it was over, he withdrew off to himself. Perhaps the shiner around his right eye had something to do with the subtle distance he kept from the other students. Whatever the case, she was glad he'd stayed behind. Now she might find out about his black eye.

"Israel, is there something on your mind?" She skirted her desk and walked back to him as the boy stood up. Nearly as tall as she, he ducked his head and nodded.

"Yes'm." He tucked his hands in his pockets. "I mean, no ma'am. Not really."

Amused by his nervousness, Amy bit back a smile and waited.

"I just wanted to tell you ... the last teacher told me I shouldn't come to school." Amy gasped. Israel took a breath and brushed his dark hair off his forehead. "That I was too far behind now and I should get a job. I thought you should know, 'case you agreed with him."

Hope burned in his bright, young face, and Amy's heart melted. "Israel, I wouldn't say you are behind. I learned today that the children in this school are at many different levels. If you want to stay and learn, you are more than welcome in my classroom."

He straightened up instantly with the encouragement. "My pa thinks I can't do more. He thinks it's a waste of time, reading with the little ones. But Ma read to me a lot."

Amy treaded lightly here, not wanting to contradict a father she didn't know, but crushing the boy's hunger to learn was not acceptable. "I think a man can accomplish anything he sets his mind to."

Israel glowed like she'd lit a torch on the inside of his soul. "My ma used to say that same thing exactly." He grabbed the baseball from inside his desk and hugged it to his chest, breathless with, Amy hoped, eagerness to learn. "She had pretty hair like you. I miss her." Israel spun and bounded from the room before she could reply.

Amy felt ... exhilarated. Her first day in Evergreen, and she not only adored her students, but thought she might have a real calling here. Especially for young Israel. She watched the boy from the door of the school. He jogged on his way, tossing his baseball into the air and catching it, over and over. Just before he rounded the corner to disappear behind a huge boulder, he stopped the ball and waved. Amy waved back. Grinning from ear to ear, he ducked behind the rock, to follow, she assumed, a road out of town.

All right, Lord, she thought, *I'm believing You will bring something good out of what happened to me. Please help me to help these children, especially Israel.*

Exhaling softly, she turned her attention in the opposite direction. Toward town. Evergreen was less than a half-mile away but tall, ponderosa pines and one rolling hill blocked her view of it. She listened, but couldn't make out any sounds other than the birds overhead, along with an early fall breeze dancing in the trees. A lovely afternoon ... yet the quiet, the isolation, began to prey on her nerves, stalking her like a panther. She was alone. Vulnerable. Sweat beaded on her upper lip.

God, will I ever get over this? Can't I be alone for one minute without feeling like I'm going to faint from fear? Please, God, calm me ...

She'd barely finished the prayer when Susan drove over the hill. She waved and pulled right up to the door. "Your ride, Madame."

Amy smiled and curtsied, amazed at her relief. "Thank you, Susan. I'll just get my shawl and lock up."

Moments later, Amy climbed into the wagon and settled next to her hostess, her good mood restored. She refused to dwell on the irrational relief swelling in her. She needed to learn to be alone again, but right now, she would wallow in Susan's company.

"How was your first day?" the woman asked, popping the reins.

"Much, much better than I dared hope. I adore the children. They're all so well-behaved."

"Good, God-fearing folks in Evergreen. We try to raise 'em right."

"That's obvious." She thought again of the young, mostly eager, faces of her students, ranging in age and education, even cultural backgrounds. She had the German Degrafenfreidt girls, Tommy—an Irish lad, and the two Sanchez boys from Mexico, to name a few. Most of the children helped their parents by working as cowboys, store clerks, and farmers, but their destinies were known only to God. She was honored to play a part in opening doors for them, which made her think of Israel. "I do have one student I'm particularly interested in teaching. I may even tutor him. Do you know Israel Packett?"

Susan's face darkened and her lips thinned.

Amy was surprised by the abrupt change. "I'm sorry, did I say something I shouldn't have?"

"No, it's not you. Not even the boy. It's his pa. A tough-talkin' blowhard who drinks too much and hates the world. He's spent time in every jail in Wyoming. He beats Israel for the fun of it. Ben had a run-in with him just a couple of weeks ago."

Amy was horrified. That explained Israel's shiner. Perhaps that was why he was so intent on schooling. An education could be a way out of this town and away from his father—another violent, worthless human being, like the men who had attacked her. Would she have to have any dealings with Mr. Packett?

"Is the father dangerous?" she asked hesitantly.

Susan pondered the question a moment before answering. "Amy, I know you have concerns. Based on everything you've been through, including what happened at the train station, I understand your fears, but I give you my word that Evergreen is as safe a town as you will find anywhere."

"Then what were those two ruffians doing in town with the marshal in the first place?"

"A posse caught up with them. It just so happened Evergreen was the closest jail. This is Dent's territory, so he swung by to pick 'em up." Susan sighed. "How I've missed him. We used to see so much of him. He grew up here, you know."

"No, I didn't." Disinterested, Amy studied the neatly painted, pristine businesses on Main Street. A bakery, millinery, dress shop, law office, all perfectly charming, perfectly mundane. A good place to grow up. Yet she saw a threat in every face that watched her, every stranger who stared too long. Except the children. She was comfortable with them.

"You mentioned this morning you haven't slept well." Susan clucked at the horse, unhappy with his pace. "Doctor Phillips instructed Henry to give you a sleeping aid if you request it."

"No," Amy shook her head firmly. "I'm done with the laudanum. I took it for two weeks and despised how it made me feel. I still have nightmares, but at least not every night now." Which begged the question of how had she slept the other night? She recalled the moment of breathless fear, of sickening panic, now almost erased by warm, safe daylight. A picture of Evergreen, cloaked in moonlight, flashed in her mind, but she didn't remember why it was there.

It felt to her like there should be more, something she *should* remember ...

"The nightmares should fade in time. Are you still having anxiety attacks?"

"The one at the train station was the first in a while, but I still feel so ... threatened. I was afraid I would be waiting on you at the school and I didn't want to be alone. Something that never bothered me before ..." she trailed off, sad over the loss of the spirited, confident woman she used to be. Oh, yes, she was a bookworm, but she'd been a happy one. Alone but not lonely; quiet but not timid. She took off her glasses and cleaned them with her skirt, merely for something to do.

"Doctor Phillips's prognosis is very good for you, Amy." Gray tufts of hair, loosened from her bun, swirled around her forehead. Smiling, she tried tucking a hair back in place, as her faded green eyes, keen with compassion, met Amy's. "He said you're quite resilient."

Amy couldn't help but return the smile, though hers felt weak and shaky.

"You will heal from this, dear. I can't think of a better town for rejuvenation."

Amy hoped so. "The children, I think, may help me more than anything. I feel so ... at peace with them. Their joy and their innocence, it's like they're healing me."

She expected a doubtful expression from Susan. Instead, the woman's smile widened, lifting her chubby cheeks. "Well, they are a blessing from the Lord," she winked at Amy "Reckon that means they're medicine, too."

They rode on in silence for a moment before Susan broached another subject. "The mayor was surprised to hear you'd arrived early, and wanted to host a dinner for you tonight. Henry persuaded him to postpone it for a bit. I hope that was a wise decision."

"Oh, you have no idea how wise." The mere mention of a dinner with strangers, all staring at her, asking questions about things back in Ohio, made Amy want to crawl under a rock. "I'd prefer to put that off for as long as possible."

"I can understand. Also, the town normally hosts a party to celebrate the new teacher. I hope we didn't overstep our bounds, but we suggested they combine that with the harvest festival. Henry believes in a month you'll be so comfortable in Evergreen, you'll be singing and dancing like nothing—" she stopped mid-sentence.

Amy heard the unfinished thought. "Like nothing ever

happened? I hope you're right. I'd like to be myself again, and quit jumping at shadows."

Susan reached over and took Amy's hand. "You will. God will heal you … in His time and His way, but He will heal you."

CHAPTER 7

*D*ent threw his saddlebags onto the cot in cell number one and turned to the empty sheriff's office. In Evergreen.

Might as well be Timbuktu.

He rested his hands on his hips and scolded himself for being surly. He knew better. Ben would have given him a hard time over this attitude. Ben would have told him to take this like a man.

Ben.

Dent trudged over to the desk and sat down. The pile of wanted posters, sitting as he'd left them a few days ago, struck him as pointless. Ben was gone. Pa had been dead for almost eight years now. Nothing Dent could do now would bring either one of them back.

Scared by the thought, he sat up and started rifling through the posters. He'd spent too long on this road. He wasn't going to abandon it now. He'd finish this and deal with what came next ... later.

The front door squeaked and he looked up to see Doc's

annoyingly cheerful face. The man grinned at him. "Saw you ride by. Thought I'd stop in and say hi."

Dent waved him in without any enthusiasm. Not only had Doc gotten Dent stuck in this town, he would be bringing the details about Ben's funeral arrangements. He was growing less and less fond of the good doctor's company.

Doc sat down and crossed one leg over the other. "Things go well in Cheyenne?"

"Depends. The hanging went fine. I'm suspended." Doc's brows lifted in surprise. Dent frowned. "I guess you don't know anything about that? Or that I've been appointed interim sheriff in Evergreen, while Judge Lynch investigates Ben's shooting?"

Doc admired his fingernails for a moment. "Well, Judge Lynch and I exchanged a few telegrams back and forth." He looked up. "I won't deny it. I merely made a recommendation. His choice to follow through."

Dent fingered a Wanted poster for "Prickly" Bill Smott. Outlaws and their nicknames. "I'm to do this job without pay, but I can keep my other duties. Guess I won't starve while I wait to find out if I get my badge back or not."

"Dent, speaking of next steps," Doc slid forward to the edge of the chair. "Ben's funeral is tomorrow. Eleven o'clock." Dent let a soft sigh escape. "He wanted to be buried on the ranch," Doc continued. "Afterward, I thought Susan and I could maybe help you go through some of his personal belongings."

Dent had used Ben's guestroom less and less these last few years, but, as he recalled, the place was pretty spartan. Didn't seem like there'd be much there to go through, but he shrugged. "Sure. Thank you."

Doc nodded, leaned back again in the chair, and crossed his ankles. "One other thing. The mayor isn't too happy with you taking up residence in Evergreen, even if you are just temporary."

"What's his problem with me?" Dent didn't recall having ever met the mayor.

"He's afraid *trouble* will follow you." Doc waved his hand, as if dismissing the concern. "And he thinks you're too young for the responsibilities that come with the position. I say don't put any stock in what he says. He's always sniffing around for something to worry over. But he's insisting on coming to the house as soon as possible to meet Miss Tate ... and he wants you there as well."

Dent drummed his fingers on Prickly Bill's picture. *What responsibilities? Keep the peace, arrest miscreants.* He could do that in his sleep, *especially* in Evergreen. "A monkey could sheriff this town." He flinched. "No reflection on Ben. It's just ... I've chased down some pretty mean *hombres*. Evergreen should be a cakewalk."

A funny, almost mischievous, expression passed over Doc's face and he stood. "Then I reckon you'll die of boredom. But not before dinner with the mayor. I'll let you know when it's scheduled."

---

*D*ent sat in the front row of the little church and barely paid any attention to the hushed whispers. The sight of the casket threw him for a loop. Ben and Pa had been U.S. Marshals together for nigh unto sixteen years. They had been as close as any brothers and Ben was in almost every childhood memory Dent could dredge up.

Ben's wife, along with their son, had stepped out of the picture long ago. Consequently, Ben had spent most Christmases with the Hernandezes. And Easters. And birthdays. He never stayed long, though, as he lived for the hunt. He wouldn't allow Dent to call him 'uncle', but the request from a young boy of only six had put a smile on the lawman's face.

And now that man—a good man who had been like a father to Dent, was dead. He squeezed his eyes shut against the painful rush of guilt. If he'd only been a blink-of-an-eye faster than Needles ...

Someone, most likely Doc, squeezed his shoulder. The squeak in the pews told Dent the mourners were standing, but he couldn't. He couldn't stand. He wanted to kneel at Ben's casket and beg his forgiveness.

A delicate whiff of perfume, something sweet and light, like the scent of a rose maybe, wafted across his soul. Calmed him. Miss Tate flipped open a hymnal. She glanced down, smiled at him with cool compassion, and hesitantly offered to share her book.

Although he had no intention of singing, Dent slowly rose to his feet and leaned in enough to at least see the words.

It is Well with My Soul ...

Only it wasn't, and likely never would be again.

CHAPTER 8

From the back seat of the surrey, Dent stared past Susan's and Henry's shoulders at the wagon in front of them, the wagon with Ben's pine coffin in it, leading a somber procession out to the ranch. Every time that pine box shifted, grief stabbed him soul-deep and he had to grit his teeth against the knot in his throat.

The ride out to Ben's for the burial was a dismal, lonely expedition, even with Henry and Susan, but, amazingly, Miss Tate's presence beside him and the gentle aroma of flowers brought him a little peace. Antsy, he shifted in the back seat and rolled a tense shoulder. Honestly, he wished the woman had stayed in town. He dreaded Ben's burial more than he could say, and didn't want to share the experience with a stranger. He felt too ... vulnerable. For some reason he couldn't explain, he didn't want her to see him that way.

Stealing a glance at her now, he was unexpectedly amused to see her pretty face aglow with wonder over the towering, snow-capped Lander Mountains. "I take it the landscape is a little different in Ohio?"

"You could say that."

He nodded, but Ben's coffin drew him back and sobered him. The desire for talk, small or otherwise, left him. What he wouldn't give to be past all this.

An hour later, Dent tossed a farewell shovel of dirt on his friend's grave, and he and Doc laid their tools in the back of the wagon. He nodded at the pastor, giving him permission to finish the burial.

"Dent, my door is always open," Pastor Wills clutched his hand and smiled. "Any time you want to talk, come on by. I promise I'll try to go light on the fire and brimstone."

Dent couldn't muster even a chuckle, but shook the pastor's hand. "You sure you don't want some help?" He motioned to the grave.

"No, son, you go on. I'll do this."

Dent and Doc, followed by Susan and Miss Tate, strode somberly down the hill through dry September grass to Ben's house. Taking a breath, he surveyed his friend's home ... now his.

A simple, one-level log cabin, a wide porch protected it on two sides. Dent grinned at the pipes and jars of tobacco that covered a table next to a rocking chair. He suspected Ben had spent most of his free time out here, enjoying the view and admiring his land.

"If it's all right, Dent," Susan touched his elbow, "Miss Tate and I will gather up Ben's clothes. You can't fit them, and the benevolence committee at church could certainly use them."

"That's fine." Dent raised his hat, ran his hands through his hair, and dropped the Stetson back in place. "Reckon I'll go through his papers."

"I'll put your horse up, Dent, and bring in your saddlebags."

"Thanks, Doc," Dent mumbled. He was lost in thought. How many years since he'd been here? The place hadn't changed much; just a little more weather-beaten was all. His first few years as a U.S. Marshal, he'd come by to see Ben pretty regularly. Somewhere along the line, the visits happened less and less frequently. He probably hadn't slept in Ben's extra room in, what, three years?

"Five."

Susan startled him, and he blinked.

"Five years since you've been here."

That long?

Slogging through mud would have been easier than trekking through Ben's simple, clean, almost sterile, home. A few Indian rugs hung on the walls, a Winchester rested above the fireplace, a regulator clock ticked forlornly in the kitchen. Ben had not been a collector of personal items or dust-catchers. A gun rack adorned the wall next to the door and that was about it.

A gloomy weight settled on Dent, but he forged ahead with the task. He let himself into Ben's guest bedroom, Doc following. The room was simple, austere. No curtains hung from the single window, and a worn wool blanket with an Indian design covered the bed. A desk—neat, orderly, barely used—was pushed into the corner. Once upon a time, this had been Dent's place to flop any time, day or night, covered in trail dust or blood.

"He moved his desk in here. Said he wanted to get some use out the room," Doc explained from behind him. "He spent most nights at the jail, though, 'specially after you quit dropping by."

Wincing, Dent settled at the desk, pulled out the center drawer. "Am I searchin' for anything in particular?" He rifled through an assortment of pencils, keys to the jail, and a bag of licorice candy.

Doc sat down on the bed. "You want to find things like tax documents, deeds, bills of sale. Things like that."

"All right," he sighed, resigned. "All right then."

Dent read the signature at the bottom of the deed then laid the document down. After two hours of digging through personal letters, tax receipts, and legal papers, one thing was abundantly clear to him. "He owns the ranch. Here's the deed. He paid off the mortgage two years ago."

Doc, still sitting on Ben's bed, laid down the documents he'd been perusing and nodded. "And the property taxes appear to be up to date. He left you sitting pretty." He rifled through a stack of papers to his left and pulled one out. "And this one says he had five hundred and forty two dollars in the bank. That's yours too."

Dent leaned back and rubbed his neck. A ranch, two geldings, and $542 were all Ben had in the world, and now those earthly possessions were his. Didn't seem fitting. He wasn't deserving of even the most meager inheritance. He shifted in the chair, and his boot kicked something that sounded tinny and hollow.

Curious, he peered down and saw the end of a metal box barely poking out from beneath the desk. It would have been hidden, safely tucked away, if he hadn't bumped it. And that made him more curious. He pulled the box from its hiding place and set it on the desk. An old, gray, tin cartridge box was all.

"What you got there?" Doc asked, setting aside his papers and coming to the desk.

"I dunno." Dent pried the lid off and held his breath for a moment when he saw the newspaper clipping. *U.S. Marshals Gunned Down in Evergreen.* Old wounds ached as he passed the yellowed newspaper clipping to Doc then reached in to see what else the box held. He pulled out a .44 brass shell, a bill of sale for a grade mare sold by Toby White to Tom Newcomb, names Dent didn't recognize, and, finally, a folded, yellowed piece of paper. Dent opened it slowly.

He held a Wanted poster for this Tom Newcomb, aka Tom Newsome, aka Tom Newly. A bounty of $1000 blazed atop the paper. The photo showed a surly, squint-eyed, dark-haired man with a deep scar across his throat.

An idea simmering in Dent's head, he read the bandit's description. *Age, 23, height five feet, ten inches. Dark hair. Blue eyes. Even features. Marks: a noticeable scar on his throat easily hidden with a bandanna. Also, scars on ... both wrists from work on a chain gang ...*

His shock must have shown on his face.

"Dent, what is it?"

He shook his head and finished reading.

No known companions. Newcomb is wanted for the murder of Union Pacific foreman, Horace Brewer. He may be linked to other murders as well. The order was signed by Judge John J. Lynch. March 1, 1882.

Six years ago.

Absently, he handed the poster to Doc, his mind spinning like a paper pinwheel. There was only one reason Ben would have that Wanted poster. He knew, or at least strongly suspected, this Newcomb fella had killed Pa. *But why hide the poster?* He ran his fingers over the lid. The dust coated his fingers.

The box had sat there for who-knows-how-long. Had Ben given up? Stopped searching?

"Son," Doc folded the poster and placed it back in its casket. "Ben laid this aside." Doc placed the items one by one back into the box. "You should, too. Let this go."

"Let it go?" Dent would sooner quit breathing. "Ben knew who killed Pa. I've got a name now, and a description. This is the best lead I've had. *Why* did Ben let it go? Why didn't he ever tell me?"

Doc clasped his hands and sat back down on the bed. "I don't know, son. I only know that if Ben had it hidden, he meant for it to stay that way."

CHAPTER 9

The sheriff's burial was a small, solemn affair, attended only by the pastor, the Woodruffs, Sheriff Hernandez, and Amy. She was an intruder in the affair and knew it, but when the Woodruffs had asked her if she wanted to come, she couldn't say no. Otherwise, what would she do with herself in town? Wander the streets of Evergreen alone? Cower in her room? So, she'd chosen to intrude.

At least she'd been of some assistance with sorting the meager supply of clothes the man had. She dropped the last box into the back of the wagon and grabbed the quilt draped on the side. She helped Susan spread the blanket and a fine picnic supper down near a small, gently bubbling creek.

Enjoying the warmth of the late afternoon sun, Pastor Wills and the Woodruffs reminisced about Sheriff Hayes, recalling funny stories, interesting arrests, his good nature, and unequaled beef brisket. Sheriff Hernandez nodded, offered a few memories of his own, but in brief, short sentences. He struck Amy as less grief-stricken than *distracted*. She berated herself for the unkind thought. People grieved in different ways. She needed to check her judgmental attitude.

"Do you remember that time, Dent," Pastor picked up an ear of corn, "when you got in trouble for soaping old Mr. Vicker's store?"

The Woodruffs laughed and Sheriff Hernandez hung his head, grinning. "I do recall that."

"Your pa and Ben brought you to me and asked me to give you a fire-and-brimstone sermon about Hell and where your wicked ways would lead."

"I remember. I hid under my bed for a week."

The pastor chuckled and his face softened. "Yes, I put a little too much fire in the conversation, I suspect, just to placate your pa. He wanted you scared good."

"It worked ... for a while."

Awkward laughter faded to a more awkward silence.

Susan rescued them. "Dent, do you remember the first time you rode out with your pa and Ben? When you came by the house? What you told me?"

Sheriff Hernandez spun his fork in a heap of mashed potatoes and slipped further down Memory Lane, a bit unwillingly, Amy guessed by the dip in his brow.

"I told you I wasn't sure I wanted to be a lawman. And that I was scared."

"Reckon you got over that, too" Doc said in a strange, almost bitter, tone.

"Reckon I did."

Amy envied the sheriff and his courage.

She assessed the plain but clean ranch house several yards away, comparing it to the teacher's cottage. Her new home would be ready soon and she would be spending her nights there ... alone. A man like Dent Hernandez probably wasn't scared of staying all the way out here on his own. He probably wasn't afraid of anything at all.

Susan seemed to sense all the heavy thoughts and cleared her throat. "Dent, when you're done, why don't you show Miss Tate the property? We've got time before we head out."

That dip in his brow deepened, communicating plenty, and Amy shook her head. "No, that's all right. He doesn't have to. I've seen enough."

The sheriff tossed his chicken bone down on the plate. "Wouldn't want to bore her, Susan. Miss Tate probably has some books she needs to get back to."

Amy frowned. She hadn't meant to be rude but his response was unnecessarily brusque. "I only meant, Sheriff, that I'm sure you'd rather not waste your time. You don't seem very pleased about your inheritance, after all."

Scowling, Sheriff Hernandez ran his tongue over his teeth in irritation, as if she'd gone a hair too far commenting on his business. Perhaps she had, but before she could apologize, he rose to his feet and wiped his hands on his pants. "I'll bring the surrey around, Doc. I expect you all are ready to head back."

The older man rose as well, though slowly, and stiffly, rubbing a knee before he stood all the way up. "I'll help you."

As the two walked away, Amy heard Doc scolding the young man. "Honestly, son, you've been chasing outlaws for so long, you've forgotten how to be mannerly. You're as prickly as a porcupine."

The sheriff's frustrated but hushed response was lost on the pleasant fall breeze. Susan tsked-tsked, and shook her head as she watched the men walk away. "He's right. Dent doesn't know much about simple pleasantries and small talk anymore. He's become a hard man. Not the boy I knew." She slapped her thighs to break the spell of melancholy. "Before we clean up, let's take a walk."

"And I'll be heading back to town." Pastor Wills dropped his napkin on his plate. "Susan, as always, a fine meal. Thank you." He shifted to Amy. "Miss Tate, I hope to see you in church."

"I'll be there."

Amy enjoyed the late afternoon sun on her face, the tickle of the September breeze, and the wispy clouds above. Swanton seemed a hundred years away, and beneath all this sky, she could almost pretend that one fateful night was too.

"There's a lot to him," Susan said, tugging on Amy's sleeve and pulling her off the trail toward the lone pine up on the hill. The spot where they had buried Ben. "Dent was only sixteen when his mother died, and he was eighteen when his father and Ben were bushwhacked."

"Bushwhacked?" Amy had never heard the word.

"Attacked. Drifters, we assume. Trying to steal horses. Will and Ben rode up on 'em by sheer coincidence. Ben survived." Susan reached down and plucked daisies and columbine as they strolled. "Both of them were only two days from retirement." Her fingers worked as she talked, arranging the flowers into a lovely bouquet. "Dent worked on a ranch outside of town, but from time to time he rode with Will and Ben, when they needed an extra gun."

They strolled past the pine, past Ben's lonely grave, then a few feet further on, Amy saw the two headstones, together but forlorn, in the tall grass. She wandered up to them and read the names. William Arturo Hernandez and Etta Mae Lancaster Hernandez. The sheriff's parents.

"The day after the shooting, Dent went straight to Judge Lynch for a job in the U.S. Marshals. Less than a week later, he sold his pa's ranch and hasn't stepped foot on the place since. Ben and Will's spreads were side by side, so, when

Dent sold out, Ben bought this one acre for them." Susan motioned to the graves as she knelt down then placed the bouquet on Etta Mae's grave. "Etta Mae and I were best friends. I miss those days."

At a loss, but truly sympathetic to Susan's pain, Amy touched her shoulder. "I'm sorry."

"I'm more sorry for what their son has turned into. Revenge is why he's a marshal, and it's making him into a man with a cold heart. He's hunting for Will's killer."

"For eight years?" A thousand stories danced through Amy's mind. Tales of revenge, hate, violence. Poison. A quote from Victor Hugo surfaced. "Every blade has two edges," she said softly. "He who wounds with one wounds himself with the other."

Susan didn't move for a moment then she nodded. "Yes." She climbed to her feet and dusted off her dress. "Yes, and I believe he's just about cut himself to pieces."

CHAPTER 10

Grinning like the Cheshire cat, Susan opened the door for Amy and gestured to the little log cabin's entrance. "Your new home, Miss Tate."

Amy struggled against the habit of wringing her hands and dropped them to her side. She smiled at Susan instead, and stepped into the two-room cabin.

Several women, giggling and twittering like birds, floated out from the kitchen area, each holding a gift or a plant. "Welcome, Miss Tate," an older, skinny woman said, stepping away from the flock. "I'm Mrs. Hannah Banks, president of the Benevolence Committee. We're so glad to have you in Evergreen."

"Oh, why, thank you."

"Please, take a gander," another woman spoke from behind Mrs. Banks. "I made your curtains."

Red paisley curtains hung from the windows, and orange and yellow dried flowers rested along the log hearth that jutted out from the fieldstone fireplace. Hooked rugs in bright colors littered the floor. A vase filled with more flowers added reds and purples to the little kitchen table.

Amy noticed newly-crocheted pot holders hanging from a hook on the wood stove. No details had been overlooked in making the cabin a truly warm and inviting home.

And it terrified her. Trying to be gracious, she swallowed her fear and nodded at the ladies. "It is lovely. So inviting. Thank you ... thank you all."

"Here," Susan stepped forward. "Let me introduce you to all my crafty little helpers."

Amy tried to pay attention, but the names and the faces blurred. The women were kind and gracious, eager to have her over for tea or to help with projects, but Amy felt her smile becoming more and more forced. She needed quiet, yet she was terrified of being alone.

After half an hour, Susan discreetly suggested everyone go home, and she walked the ladies to the door. Amy waved, thanked them all again, and promised to come by for a visit soon. She would, too, someday.

Susan closed the door and faced Amy, wearing a sympathetic smile. "I know that was a lot to take in, but they sincerely want you to feel welcome."

"And I do." The unspoken *but* hung in the air.

"Dear, if it's too soon ..." Susan's gentle voice calmed Amy, reassuring her she still had a choice.

"You've housed me for a month. That's enough. I want to try, at least."

Susan stepped up and clutched her arm. "That's right. You try. If you get scared, you just run right back to our house. I don't care what time of day or night."

Amy grimaced. She could see herself pounding on the Woodruffs' door in the wee hours of the night, half-dressed, hair a mess. She could see it all too easily and shivered. "No —I mean, I'll try my best not to do that."

"All right then," Susan patted her shoulder. "Let's get your things from the wagon. We'll get you settled, then I'll go start dinner. Henry or Dent will fetch you at six."

"Dent?"

Susan's forehead creased with worry. "I'm sorry. Is he too much of a stranger still? I suppose that demeanor of his doesn't exactly engender affection. Henry and I will fetch you then."

Amy chewed on her bottom lip. Susan had to cook. Doctor Woodruff should be there to assist or greet the mayor. They couldn't hold her hand forever. She had to deal with her fears. After all, she'd managed to come all this way on the train, surrounded by strangers. The recollection made her queasy. The ladies' room had been her sanctuary when real or imagined stares became too bold or curious. If her heart started galloping or sweat broke out on her brow, off she'd go to hide in the small room.

She'd managed to cross the country without fainting anywhere along the way. And she'd sat across from the sheriff at the dinner table almost every night for a month. Surely, she could ride two blocks with the man, whether he liked it or not. She suspected he wouldn't. He'd barely spoken to her during their evenings at the Woodruffs. Yet, somehow, she'd achieved a certain level of comfort with him, due to his vocation, she assumed.

"If the sheriff wouldn't mind too much, I believe I can ride with him, which would leave you free to get ready for your guests."

The corners of Susan's mouth twitched, as if she was fighting a smile. "Fine, then. I'll send Dent after you."

One gander at who had become the mayor of Evergreen made Dent want to burn down the town. Ed Coker sat in the parlor with Doc, enjoying a fat cigar by the fireplace. He wore a tailored suit, salt-and-pepper hair stylishly slicked back, and the whitest silk shirt Dent had ever laid eyes on. A square jaw and broad shoulders added to the portrait of success.

Coker had come to town eight years ago, with nothing to his name but a broken-down nag. He'd smiled his way into businesses, and in the course of only a few days had run up tabs all over Evergreen. Job hunting hadn't been on his agenda, as he'd hardly ever left the saloon. He'd had a dust-up with Pa just a few days before the shooting. Something about those unpaid debts, if Dent remembered correctly.

In the end, Ben had cleared Coker as a suspect in the shooting, due to a solid alibi. Dent hadn't been around much after that, so his surprise at the man's political fortune was colossal.

With a raised brow, Coker surveyed Dent top to bottom. Dent pulled the Stetson from his head and ran his fingers through damp hair, glad he'd taken the time to spiff up a bit, but annoyed he cared. "Coker."

Coker smiled, but there was no warmth behind it. "Dent." The mayor lifted his muscular frame from the chair and reached for Dent's outstretched hand. "Good to see you. And it's *Mayor* Coker now."

As they shook hands, each man took an instant to size up the other, like bulls eyeing trouble. Or, perhaps, a rival? Dent remembered the man had a streak of competitiveness, which had led to a few fights in the saloon, prior to this *respectable* path.

"Last time I saw you, Dent, you were covered in horse shi

—er, I mean, manure. Glad to see you've chosen slightly cleaner work."

Dent had no reply for the veiled slice—at least nothing polite—so he moved on to Doc, now standing as well, and reached for his hand. "Doc."

"Susan's made your favorite, country-fried steak."

Dent rubbed his stomach. "Aw, that'll hit the spot all right."

"Doc," the mayor folded his tails in and re-took his seat, motioning to the collection of spirits on the credenza. "I suggest a toast to our new sheriff."

"I'll go along with that." Doc strode to the counter, where a decanter of brandy waited.

The mayor pointed at the chair across from him. "Dent, let's you and me hammer out a few details of this *interim* position."

"Happy to," he lied.

Doc passed the drinks to them and held his glass aloft. "To our new sheriff. May he find many, many reasons to stay in Evergreen."

A twitch in the corner of his mouth made Dent wonder if Doc was trying to annoy him ... or the mayor. A twitch in the politician's brow—almost a grimace—answered the question. Amused, Dent drank the shot to hide a grin.

The mayor forged ahead, maintaining his cool air. "Dent, I hear you're going to sell Ben's ranch. I'd like to be first in line for it, especially if you're going to sell it as fast as you did your pa's. What's your asking price?"

Dent absolutely wanted to sell Ben's place. He wanted his badge back, and he wanted out of Evergreen. But selling to Coker just felt all wrong. "I haven't quite decided yet." He ignored Doc's raised eyebrow. "If I decide to sell, I'll let you know."

The mayor seemed to take a moment to digest that then shrugged it off. "All right, let's discuss your schedule."

"My schedule?"

"Congressman Carey will be stopping by for a brief campaign visit next week. The town leaders, including you now, will be meeting him at the station. I'm not sure of the date yet, but I think," the mayor rubbed his chin, pondering, "yes, next month, the gents from the railroad are coming in. You're to take them up to the Gilmer Crossroads, so they can see where that spur line is s'posed to go. And I know you have one eviction to perform as soon as possible. Oh, and a pie contest to judge." The mayor finished with a cold smile, "Your calendar is filling up."

Dent's hand strangled the shot glass, and he stood slowly. Doc had remained standing and, when their eyes met, the physician wisely inched back a hair. Dent strode over and set his glass on the credenza and kept his back to the room. With every passing minute, he was loving Evergreen more and more. One of the last scoundrels to see his father alive was now the mayor of this worthless hole. What he thought about that and this new position's duties couldn't be spoken in polite company, and he needed a moment to rein in his mouth.

"Anything else, *Mayor*?"

"Dent?" Susan's voice from the doorway brought him around. "Would you mind fetching Miss Tate? Dinner's almost ready."

"Gladly." Tossing a scowl at Doc, he marched from the room, but didn't miss the smile playing on Coker's lips.

"Wagon's out back, ready to go," Doc called. Dent ignored him and stomped to the front door.

"Dent, wait, please," Susan's voice brought him up short and he turned to her. "Dent, I don't know what's got you so agitated, but would you please try to be more ... *civil* to Miss Tate? I'm afraid your brusqueness could ... upset her."

All kinds of messages, maybe warnings, seemed to run wild on Susan's round, chubby face, but he couldn't read any of them. He reached behind her and lifted his hat from the wall hook. "She *is* kind of ... fragile, isn't she?"

He tried to piece it together: her concern that the town wasn't as peaceful as someone had promised her, Doc's veiled suggestion that folks in town didn't know much about her. And he'd had the sense more than once that much of the dinner conversation at the Woodruffs' had skated around something. Health problems, maybe? He'd been so absorbed with his own issues that he'd barely given the woman much thought ... except for her perfume. Admittedly, it lingered some, especially when he hit the cot at the jail or on the long ride out to the ranch.

He scratched his stubbly jaw. "She got a bad heart or something?"

Susan pursed her lips and folded her arms over her generous stomach. "Or something. You've made no effort to get to know her. Can you just please try to be ... a little friendlier tonight?"

He frowned at her. "I'll give it my best shot."

That didn't seem to reassure Susan. She sighed and whispered, "Oh, dear."

CHAPTER 11

The five-minute walk from Doc's to the teacher's cottage at the edge of town didn't give Dent near enough time to shake off his fury. *A glorified conductor. I'm a stinkin', glorified conductor.*

The street was empty, and his footfalls thudded loudly on the boardwalk. The stomping seemed disrespectful to the solemn Sunday-evening quiet. The long shadows reaching across the street seemed to ask him for patience. Taking a deep breath, he slowed down, and fanned a frustrated hand over his face.

A pie contest. I have to judge a pie contest? Of all the stupid, worthless ...

His steps transformed to stomps again, and he let the sound of his boots boom down the street. How had he gone from chasing some of the toughest outlaws in the territory to glad-handing politicians and judging pastries?

He'd gotten a good friend killed—that was how.

So he would take his punishment like a man.

𝓗e raised his fist to pound on Miss Tate's door, but caught himself at the last second. *Don't scare the little rabbit.* Reined in, he tapped gently. "Miss Tate, it's Marshal—I mean, *Sheriff* Hernandez."

"Just a minute."

Lost again in his misery, Dent shuffled across the porch to lean on a post. The mountains surrounding Evergreen glowed brilliant oranges and purples in the setting sun. He realized it had been a while since he'd appreciated the Lander Mountains for their simple, rugged beauty. Truth be told, he hadn't noticed much of anything in the last eight years. If it wasn't a Wanted poster, a hoofprint along the trail, a witness's description, or an arrest warrant, it got swept to the edges of his mind.

The door opened behind him and he swung back around. For an instant, Miss Tate captured his attention, and his mouth fell open. She wore a nice-fitting, green-checked dress that hugged alluring curves and set off her blue eyes, even behind the glasses. She had her hair swept up in a kind of loose bun, but one soft curl rebelled and hung at her neck, flirting with the lace at her neckline. And something about the setting sun sure brought out a pretty golden tone in her skin.

Stunned at the direction of his thoughts, Dent took a step back and stumbled down the steps.

"Oh, my goodness!" Miss Tate squealed, reaching out for him.

Dent righted himself quickly, managing to keep from falling on his rear end, and snatched his hat off. Heat rushed to his cheeks. He tried to crush his embarrassment with a quip. "And I haven't even been drinking yet."

The concern in her face changed to fear, and she withdrew her hand. Dent flinched. "Ma'am, I'm sorry. That was a bad joke. Truth is I hardly drink at all."

She clutched her reticule in front of her like a shield. "Hardly?"

Oh, how did I get myself into this mess? The surly attitude replaced his mortification. He wasn't about to explain his drinking habits to anyone, much less this tee-totaling librarian. He motioned to the dirt walkway. "Uh, you ready, ma'am?"

She cast around for a moment. "We're walking?"

Dent froze the expression on his face, determined not to betray his irritation. "Nice evening for a walk, and it's not far at all to Doc's."

"But it will be dark on our return?"

"Yes ma'am, that usually happens when the sun sets."

Her face tightened into outright indignation. Her little chin came up, and she marched past Dent like he was a rude drunk. Scratching his nose, he replaced his hat and caught up with her. "That was impertinent of me, Miss Tate. My apologies."

She didn't deign to respond. He sighed and drummed his fingers on his thigh as they came to the boardwalk in front of the deed office. She stopped abruptly and spun on him. "Do you know why I'm here, Sheriff?"

He blinked at her, feeling like a raccoon caught breaking into the root cellar. "To teach?"

"Is that all you've been told? Doctor Woodruff, Susan, they haven't told you anything else?"

Clearly, there *was* more, as he'd suspected, but it was her secret to keep. "No ma'am."

She stared down at the reticule in her hands, hands busy squeezing the life out of the little silk bag. "I was attacked by two men back in Swanton as I was walking home one night."

Dent held his face still, but inside he grimaced. *No wonder ...*

"An off-duty police officer chased them away before ..." She sniffed and rolled a shoulder. "I'm afraid of everything now. Strangers. The dark. The idea of a moonlit walk with a handsome gentleman absolutely terrifies me." She met his gaze then, and the pain he saw behind those wire frames moved him. "I'm sorry to be such a delicate flower. I'm sure that's most annoying to a man like you."

Dent opened his mouth, but snapped it shut. Did she think *he* was handsome? But what did she mean by that last? "A man like me, ma'am?"

"Strong, self-assured, busy with justice, bored by the inconsequential. My issues must seem very silly to you. After all, I was unharmed ... mostly."

Truly, she did have much to be thankful for. She had her life, even if a part of her soul had been taken. "I guess that's one of the good things about Evergreen then, ma'am. A body can take life slow and easy here. For what it's worth, I think you're in the right place. And I'm sorry." Her mouth formed a shocked, little 'o' and he reached his hand out, trying to snatch back the comment. "No ma'am, I meant I'm sorry you *need* to be in a place like Evergreen." That wasn't right either. "I mean, I'm sorry you even—" he rid his voice of the embarrassment and offered a simple condolence, "that you even went through anything like that."

A blush rose in her cheeks as she pursed her lips and worked on a more stern expression. "I certainly hope you don't have to do much public speaking in your new position, Sheriff. It's not your gift."

Miss Tate sat down at the Woodruffs' table, and smiled stiffly up at Mayor Coker as he pushed her chair in. Dent thought the man lingered a hair too long above her. Was he actually trying to peer down her dress? His hand squeezed into a fist.

Politicians.

Puzzled that he was so annoyed by the man's behavior toward Miss Tate, Dent grabbed a biscuit and tossed it onto his plate.

The mayor had talked the poor girl's ear off from the moment she'd walked in the door, his questions verging on intrusive. Now, he sat down opposite her as they settled in for dinner, his bold gaze warning he wasn't finished. Small talk circulated for a few moments, along with the fried steak, mashed taters, and green peas, but Mayor Coker, like a bloodhound, stayed on the scent. Dent peeked during grace and saw the man tapping his fingers. Then, after waiting a few moments, to seem respectable, Dent assumed, the mayor jumped back on the trail again.

"I'm quite impressed with your library background," Coker said as he chased some green beans around his plate. "But since I was not on the search committee, I don't know specifically why you left your job. And why did you choose to come to Evergreen?"

Miss Tate reminded Dent of a deer caught in rifle sights. While she could probably take care of herself, he saw a chance to needle the swaggering buffoon that passed for an elected official.

"Mayor, I'm surprised you even have to ask that question. I hear you never let anyone forget what a spectacularly friendly and peaceful town this is. Why, we're all blessed beyond measure to be here." Dent nailed Doc across the table with a glare. "Isn't that right, Doc?" Then he pointed at Amy with his fork. "Why, a smart young lady like Miss Tate probably never even considered another town."

Doc raised a disapproving eyebrow at Dent. The mayor scowled and picked up the argument. "Dent, it *is* a wonderful town ... but it's not a perfect town."

"Yes, I've seen the rampant crime problem here. Ben wrote a lengthy report about Sam Wiles' prize stallion getting loose and destroying Bodie Trace's fence. Oh, and there was a report about a merciless gang of ruffians setting fire to some outhouses. Evergreen has its share of low-class criminals."

"Speaking of low-class," the mayor sliced into his steak, ignoring the comment. "Are you ready to handle that eviction if the Packetts aren't ready to go?"

Amy gasped. "You're going to evict the Packetts?" Her pleading gaze bounced between Dent and the mayor. "Are you talking about Israel Packett and his father?" Back to Dent with shimmering blue eyes full of hope. "You won't evict them, will you?"

"Well, I ..." Ambushed. Coker had ambushed him, and the victory glowed on the man's face. "I don't know any of the facts yet, Miss Tate." He tilted his jaw toward the mayor. "Mayor Coker sprang this on me tonight. I'll study over the case and make my own determination."

"It's no stretch," the mayor assured them. "They've got a small spread on the edge of town. Packett's wife died three years ago and the family's fallen apart."

"That's true," Doc leaned back in his chair at the head of the table and draped an arm over the spire. "Tom has been in and out of jail since Julie's death. He's keeping some bad company over in Rawlins, and is gone a lot. It's a shame. Israel's a good boy and he deserves better."

The mayor wiped his mouth and tossed his napkin on to a cleaned plate. "Packett Sr., made his mortgage payments sporadically, Dent, but now he's a hundred and forty days past due. The bank's had enough. Ben served him with three notices."

Dent leaned forward. "A hundred and forty? Then why didn't *he* evict 'em?" The mayor's silence answered the question. "Oh. Because he didn't want to."

"That's right," Coker slapped the table. "He wouldn't. It was his duty to enforce the law and he kept coming up with excuses, putting the eviction on the back burner."

"Mayor," Susan interjected in a conciliatory tone, "why don't we talk about the fall festival?"

Doc unhooked his arm and came back to the table, resting his elbows on each side of his plate. "That's a good idea." Sounding relieved at the change in subject, he dished himself a second serving of potatoes. "There are still a lot of details to work out."

Fall festivals ranked right up there with pie-judging contests, in Dent's opinion. Not making any effort to hide his boredom, he plucked another steak from the platter. Slicing off a bite, he pondered things. What was Mayor Coker really after with that jab about the eviction? Maybe he was trying to prove Dent wasn't capable of this job, as—judging by the politician's attitude—Ben hadn't been either. Or maybe he just wanted the new lawman to look bad in front of Miss Tate.

Either way, it didn't matter. Once the investigation was settled, Dent would return to the U.S. Marshal's office, or turn out and become a bounty hunter. What he did in Evergreen, how well he served the office, wouldn't affect Judge Lynch's decision ...

Or would it? Maybe Lynch needed to see Dent doing the job by the book, making a real effort at being a lawman, not a supposed vigilante with a badge. If he had to evict a family, then he had to evict them. Tom Packett didn't sound like an upstanding citizen anyway.

Dent's gaze grudgingly drifted over to Miss Tate. She clearly cared for the boy. Making the Packetts homeless wasn't going to sit easy with her. That gave him pause.

"I assume our new sheriff won't break with tradition?" The flinty humor in the mayor's voice brought Dent back to the conversation. He discovered the whole table staring at him, and Miss Tate's eyes were wider and rounder than those wire frames of hers.

He swallowed his mouthful of steak. "I'm sorry, what'd I miss?"

The mayor grinned, but there was nothing friendly in the expression. "Why, Sheriff Hernandez, it is a tradition, twelve years running. The pumpkin-carving contest. The town council forms two teams, and you and the schoolteacher form another. We compete against each other. It's all in fun." A slick smile tipped his mouth. "Silly, pointless fun."

Dent set out to hold his face perfectly still, perfectly frozen, but against his will, the slightest quiver lifted his lip into a tiny sneer. "Pumpkin carving?" He laced his fingers together. "Well ..." The mayor was working hard to get a rise out of him by bringing up these menial, frivolous duties. Surely, it wouldn't take Judge Lynch a month to conduct the investigation. Then, one way or the other, Dent was gone. That hope gave him the strength to suck up Coker's jabs. "We'll just see how things play out. I am the *interim* sheriff, Mayor. I doubt I'll be here in October."

Mayor Coker's face relaxed a little, like he was relieved. "Well, I hate to hear that you don't want to stick around in your hometown, Dent."

And Dent hated hearing a bald-faced lie.

CHAPTER 12

*A*my pulled her knife through her steak, and tried to ignore the distaste that had raced across the sheriff's face. He did not care for carving pumpkins, or perhaps he didn't care for carving one with her.

She knew she shouldn't have confessed her ... her incident. She was a weakling in his estimation now. A burdensome citizen who might call him if there was a strange noise or spider in her kitchen. Well, she would get out of the contest, tradition notwithstanding. Someone else could carve with the man, someone more to his liking. A strong, hearty pioneer woman—that was his type; a woman who feared nothing and could shoot a shotgun with one hand and roll a cigar with the other.

The gathering moved to the parlor for coffee and dessert, but Amy's mood didn't improve, and the time passed like a snail climbing uphill. She actually found herself wishing for the quiet solitude of her cottage. Anywhere Mayor Coker was not. Tension, for whatever reason, clearly brewed between him and Sheriff Hernandez, adding to her discomfort. She endured the official's ceaseless chatter and roving gaze until 8:30.

When the clock chimed the half-hour, she jumped on a break in the conversation. "Sheriff Hernandez, could I impose upon you to escort me home now? It's late, and I've grown quite tired."

He practically leaped to his feet. "Absolutely, Miss Tate."

"Aw, now, Miss Tate," Mayor Coker rose, filling the room with his overbearing stature. "I would be happy to escort you home. We could finish this delightful discussion on Poe's works."

"I've got rounds to do, Mayor," Sheriff Hernandez cut in before Amy could answer. "I start at that end of town." His lips flattened into an unfriendly line. "No sense in both of us going down there."

The two men stared at each other, a subtle challenge in their gazes, but the mayor relented with a nod and tight smile. Not a true surrender, Amy suspected. More like a pause in the battle. The two men had avoided revealing the source of their hostility. She wished she knew. The tension made her nervous and knowledge often dispelled fear. However, it was not her place to ask.

Thankfully done with the evening, she hugged Susan good night. "Thank you so very much for the lovely meal tonight." Doc rose to stand beside Susan, and Amy squeezed his hand. "The evening was wonderful. Thank you both."

"Are you sure you don't want to stay?" Susan asked cautiously.

"Truly," Doc said, returning the gentle squeeze, "You are more than welcome if you're not ... comfortable in your new accommodations."

Amy felt both Sheriff Hernandez and the mayor watching her, and shook her head. "I'm sure I'll be fine. Thank you."

"We'll still expect you every night for supper now." Susan

clutched her hands to her bosom. "I do so love cooking, and you and Dent are such lovely company."

The sheriff set his empty cup down on the coffee table with a loud clink, and touched Amy's elbow. "Miss Tate." She and the sheriff backed out of the room, saying their goodnights, the mayor sticking with them to the front door.

Amy breathed a sigh of relief when the door shut behind them. "Does he ever stop talking?" she muttered aloud as they crossed the Woodruffs' yard to the street.

A rhetorical question, she didn't expect an answer, but the sheriff had apparently also been pondering the man. "The mayor is attracted to you, Miss Tate. The fact he has a wife doesn't seem to present him with any problem."

The remark so shocked Amy that she and the sheriff were several yards down the dark street before she realized it. Quickly, her horror over one situation changed to horror over the shadows surrounding her. She inched closer to the sheriff and folded her arms against the chill. While the sheriff instilled confidence, even trust, her surroundings were a different matter. "I can honestly say, at this moment, the thought of *him* having designs on me is only slightly less frightening than this dark street."

Sheriff Hernandez drew up instantly and turned to her. Taken aback, Amy stopped as well, all but forgetting her racing heart and sweaty palms.

"I think you should be more worried about the mayor, but ..." he tilted his head, "look around you."

"What?"

"Look around."

Obediently, she cast her glance about. The little neighborhood of sweet, gingerbread homes on their right was brushed in silver moonlight. Amber lights glowed in the windows of several of them. Two hundred feet off to their left, the backside of a dozen Main Street stores sat silent and dark. Ahead of them, an owl left his seat in an oak and glided silently to a branch higher up in a cedar.

"Now, close your eyes."

Amy held her breath. In the shadows, she couldn't see the sheriff's face clearly, but she could feel his insistent gaze. Heart pounding in her chest, she found the strength to bring her eyelids down ... and darkness swallowed her.

"Now ... listen," he whispered.

His voice seemed to hang in the air, soft and reassuring. Fighting to let go of her irrational fear, at least for a moment, she ... listened. The owl hooted, announcing his new position. A man yelled *'Lotto!',* and laughter from his friends or family playing the new board game drifted to her on the breeze. Bats chirped and chatted as they swooped somewhere over-head. A horse neighed and nickered off in the distance.

"Smell anything?"

She did. The scent of hickory and pine logs burning in fireplaces tickled her nose. She caught a whiff of leather and soap ... his scent. She opened her eyes.

"Feel better?"

"Yes, I do, actually ... a little, anyway."

He started walking again and she hurried to catch up with him. "How did you know that would help?"

"Aw," he shrugged, "something a U.S. Marshal told me once about getting your bearings. The familiar ... *grounds* you."

She could see that, but she could also still imagine someone hiding behind a tree up ahead. If she dwelt on it—the fear, the shortness of breath, the icy palms—it would all come back.

"How long have you been a U.S. Marshal?" Talking might distract her.

"This was my eighth year."

"I guess it's exciting and challenging, roaming all over the territory, capturing murderers and horse thieves."

"Challenging, to say the least. I've been shot three times and stabbed five. I sleep too often on the ground, in the cold. Sometimes I go weeks without company. I've even nearly starved to death once."

"Were you after someone? The time you starved, I mean."

"Yep. And I got him."

Amy heard the pride—or vengeance—in his voice and thought again of the Victor Hugo quote. *Every blade has two edges* ... "You have a passion for what you do."

"You could say that."

Or might he say obsession? Not familiar enough with the man to press further, she changed the subject. "I understand you grew up here. Do you really dislike it as much as you say?"

"More."

She exhaled and laced her fingers in front of her. "Oh. Well, I suppose it's a good thing you're only the interim sheriff then. Why is that; if you don't mind my asking?"

"I was suspended from the marshals, pending the investigation into Ben's death. This is ... punishment."

"Punishment? His death wasn't your fault. That man shot the sheriff."

"With my gun."

Amy couldn't argue that point, but it wasn't fair that the sheriff took any of the blame for the shooting. Sometimes, things just happened. Although she didn't suppose he wanted to hear that, as the observation was less than helpful. She stole a quick glance at him. Though he tried to hide it, the burden of all this—the death of a friend, the suspension— weighed on him. No wonder he was withdrawn and solemn.

"And the mayor prattled on about a pumpkin-carving contest as if it were life or death."

"Which will be his misfortune, if he keeps it up."

His warning for the mayor silenced her for a moment. She decided he was missing some positives about the situation. "It's absurd to you, isn't it? The simple, menial things a small-town sheriff has to do. But these things help build a community, engender trust, portray you as a man who is ... a servant of the people," she said gently.

His walk slowed a little and he shoved his hands into his pockets. He watched his feet for the next several steps, and Amy acknowledged she'd overstepped her bounds. "I'm sorry. It's really none of my business. You can certainly handle the position of sheriff without my input."

"Yes, I can." He removed his hat, scratched his head, and dropped the hat back into place. "But I would rather hear advice from you than that smiling, conceited peacock."

"Oh, the mayor," her stomach rolled, and she placed a hand over it.

"I meant it when I said you should be concerned about him. A person can change, I suppose, but when he first came to Evergreen, he was a blue-ribbon troublemaker. He tried to run a couple of confidence games. That's when Pa stepped in and threatened to arrest him."

"Was your father the sheriff of Evergreen? I thought he was a U.S. Marshal."

Sheriff Hernandez rubbed his neck, as if the memories added to his burdens. "He was both. He was leaving the Marshals and planned to stay here. The town wanted him as sheriff." He kicked a rock out of his path as he meandered down the street. "Anyway, he threatened to arrest Coker if he didn't leave town. Never had a chance to follow through. He was shot the next day."

"I'm sorry." And she was. A young boy needed a father. "Did anyone question the timing of the mayor's arrival with your father's death?"

"Ben followed up on the alibi. Said it checked out."

"How did he ever become mayor?"

"Ah," Sheriff Hernandez shrugged, "from a few, thin comments Doc's made, I gather Coker doesn't mind shmoozing folks, and he likes talking up the town. The way I see it, there's not much distance between a con man and a politician anyway."

"I can certainly see the similari—" A loud, inhuman screech or howl erupted from an alley between two homes, followed by great shattering, splintering sounds. Amy yelped and clutched the sheriff's arm. He pulled her up against him, spun her away from whatever was in that alley, and then drew his gun. An instant later, a huge tomcat exploded from the shadows and streaked down the dirt road like a shooting star.

Sheriff Hernandez chuckled and dropped his side arm back into his holster. He looked down at Amy. Their eyes locked. His body tensed and her breath caught. Heat radiated from him like a furnace. She moved to push him away, but he was faster, stepping back as if *she* was on fire. "My apologies, ma'am," he said quickly, almost breathlessly.

"No, that was entirely my fault." She pulled and straightened her shirtwaist. "The scared little rabbit." The feel of his arms around her left her befuddled and a little breathless, too.

He commenced to walking again, though faster now. "That's a lie."

"Excuse me?" She scrambled to catch up with him.

"You should quit saying things like that about yourself. You'll start believing 'em. You got on a train all by yourself, and came West to a town you'd never seen before to take a job you haven't done in years. No rabbit would do that."

"No," she mumbled, strangely pleased. "I suppose not."

CHAPTER 13

*A*gainst Miss Tate's protests, Dent gave the pretty little log cabin a thorough inspection. Fingers laced in front of her, she waited in the kitchen as he surveyed the living room, peeked into her bedroom, and checked her windows. His knees kind of jittered a little when he approached her. He could still feel her in his arms, and it unnerved him. "All clear."

"Thank you, but you didn't have to."

"Yes ma'am, I know, I just thought …" *What?* He wanted her to feel safe. *Nothing wrong with that.* "Well, I thought it might give you some peace of mind."

Disarming blue eyes, only enhanced somehow by her round, metal rims and long lashes, caused a fluttery feeling in his gut. She smiled, barely a shaky little twitch of her lips. "Thank you, it does."

He licked his lips, pondering hers. How perfect and soft … Alarmed at his train of thought, he backed away and nodded. "All right then, ma'am. Have a good evening."

He dropped his hat back in place and hurried from that

pretty little log cabin as fast as his feet could carry him, while trying not to *appear* rushed.

He stopped at an oak about a hundred feet away and leaned on it, allowing its dark, heavy branches to hide him. For the life of him, he couldn't figure why he felt so unsettled. After a moment, he realized he had his hand pressed to the steel of his stomach ... to quell those butterflies.

Nah, just a little indigestion. Susan's steaks had been a touch greasy.

Liar, an inner voice scolded. Dent backed up and faced the truth.

Somehow, holding Miss Tate in his arms, protecting her from some unseen threat, had made him feel more alive in that brief instant than he had in the last eight years. She had sent fire racing through his veins. Worse, that one moment had made him sense an emptiness in his soul.

He snorted in disgust at the melodramatic, dime-novel thoughts running wild in his head, and folded his arms across his chest.

The glow in Miss Tate's front window faded and then reappeared in her bedroom window. His mind wandered back through the last several years. The gunfights and fistfights, bullet wounds and knife scars. The long hours in the saddle. The sound of the gallows. The cold. The hunger.

The loneliness.

Sometimes he did go without company for long stretches, and sometimes he visited a gal down in Lander, most often after a hanging. No commitments from either of them, just a little comfort. Dent wondered if watching a man swing made him *need* to feel the beat of his own heart ... to assure himself *he* was still alive.

Miss Tate had done that with a single touch.

Exhaling wearily, he pushed himself off the tree and

headed toward Main Street. He walked softly in the shadowy stillness, tugging on doors, peering in windows, listening for nefarious sounds. In the back of his mind, he knew he'd wind up again at that little cabin. One last check before he quit for the night.

CHAPTER 14

Dent climbed out of the cot in cell number one and stretched the kinks out of his back. If he did much more sleeping here, he was replacing that mattress. He shuffled over to the basin and poured a splash of water. Washing the sleep from his face, pushing his hair back, he wished for a cup of coffee.

The telegram from Judge Lynch sat on the dresser beside the basin, now sprinkled with droplets of water. Dent wanted to growl at the message like a chained-up dog. Lynch did not mince words. *Investigation on-going.*

So, in other words, sit tight and do your job until you're properly humbled.

But Dent wanted out of Evergreen, now more than ever. And the urgency had to do with Miss Tate. In the jarring light of day, he realized if he wasn't careful, his goals might get fuzzy. He wouldn't let that happen. He had a job to finish —with a badge or without.

A commotion at the front door brought him out of the small alcove, wiping his hands on a towel. Two men spied him and came rushing up to him, both talking at once, one shoving a dead chicken in his face.

"Sheriff, Baker's dog went after my chickens again!"

"His chickens were on my property!"

"I told him last time if it happened again—"

"You two need to get ahold of yourselves," Dent pushed the chicken down and shoved the men back, not even trying to hide his anger. "And quit waving that chicken in my face."

Blinking, the men backed up, expressions wide and shocked. Then the man holding the carcass stepped forward again, but Dent cut him off with a raised hand. "I haven't even had my coffee yet, and you come bustin' in here, acting like the world's coming to an end over what?" He glared at the lifeless bird. "A chicken."

"Well, this is the third time—"

"His flock keeps wandering onto my property. It's not my fault my dog—"

"Fence your property!"

Both men snapped their mouths shut at what Dent meant as an order, either because they'd never thought of it, or they truly expected him to do something about a chicken-killing dog. They recovered quickly from their shock and started hollering over each other again.

"I demand money for the dead chickens—"

"I ain't payin' one red cent—"

"Enough!" Dent hollered, his patience expired.

"Is there a problem here, Sheriff?"

Dent tried not to flinch at Mayor Coker's slick, and clearly amused, tone. "No problem, unless you consider I haven't had my coffee yet."

The two men backed off a bit to allow the mayor to approach. He sized up the situation and laughed. "Baker, your dog running chickens again?"

"Wiler, here, won't keep his flock penned. Cody does what comes natural."

"Gentlemen," Dent stepped in and pushed the two men to the door. "Either address the fencing suggestion, or file a formal complaint and I'll get you a court date." Resisting, they aimed pleading expressions at Coker, but Dent shoved a little harder and pushed the men right out the door. With a warning scowl, he shut the door on them.

Coker chuckled, and Dent wanted to punch the town's highest elected official square in the face. He tamped the idea down, way down, and slowly spun around. "What can I do for you, Mayor?"

"The congressman." Dent didn't react and Coker regarded him with confusion. "The congressman's train is coming in. He'll be here at 10. You didn't forget, did you? We have to make sure things are ready. Security, banners, a podium—"

"A podium?"

"Ben stores one here, since the Town Hall isn't finished yet. I need it at the train station by 9:45."

Silence settled between them. Dent wished for coffee, but didn't believe a cup was in his immediate future. "It'll be there."

The crowd at the train station buzzed and hummed with excitement, like honey bees collecting pollen. Dent had never felt like such a lackey in his whole life, and tried to disappear behind the group of town officials. Congressman Carey, a hugely rotund man, stepped off the train onto the station platform. He eyed the red-white-and-blue banners hanging from the railroad office with an arrogant tilt to his brow, and then smiled condescendingly at Mayor Coker. "It's all fine, Mayor. Thank you for having me."

"The honor is ours, Congressman."

Platitudes and insincere sentiments polluted the air as Coker took the congressman's ample arm and led him toward the podium. Along the way, he introduced the gentleman from Cheyenne to the town council, and, then, almost as an afterthought, pulled the congressman to a halt and turned him toward Dent. "And this is our interim sheriff, former U.S. Marshal, Dent Hernandez."

Abe Rotham, a dentist and town council member, stepped aside so the two men could meet. Dent tried not cringe over the politician's sweaty grip. For the congressman, the greeting was a mere formality, and he quickly returned to the reason for the visit. Most of the town had shown up, primarily out of curiosity, Dent had been told. The crowd gathered below the platform, gazed up at the pompous congressman, and listened politely.

This nonsense would be over in another ten minutes, and he would go back to being a sheriff, not a podium-moving, banner-hanging greeter. A flash exploded from a camera, the glare blinding him. His scowl betrayed his thoughts. The expression alone could get him fired from this job.

When his vision cleared, he saw Miss Tate and her whole class standing off to the side. She smiled sweetly at him, and Dent acknowledged her with a subtle smile in return. But then he frowned, irritated that he was pleased to see her. Worse, he'd let it show. She must have seen the change. She looked away quickly, to watch the congressman instead.

Dent wanted to curse over the blunder, but refrained. Why did he even care if he'd inadvertently hurt her feelings?

He *didn't* care and she would recover from the perceived slight, without any apology or explanation from him.

CHAPTER 15

*D*ent hoisted the podium up onto his shoulder and marched through the dispersing crowd. A few folks nodded or tipped their hats to him, but he didn't speak; just gave them a disinterested dip of his chin. Eventually, he'd run into someone he knew from when he was young, someone who would want to chat. Evergreen was a nice town full of nice, peaceable citizens, but Dent hadn't missed the place. At all. He missed being on the trail, chasing bandits … making a difference. Not getting caught up in … life.

He toyed for a moment with the idea of making his way over to Miss Tate, but she was scurrying off, her class in tow behind her. Should he have apologized? Maybe. Was he disappointed at missing her?

Nope.

He shook off the annoying confusion and changed direction back toward his office.

"Excuse me, ladies." Stepping up on the boardwalk, he navigated around a group of elderly women, careful not to bean them on the head with the stand, and touched the brim of his hat. The women stared, a few gawked, they all moved.

A clatter up ahead snagged his attention. Brooms seemed to dance, and then nearly take flight as a young boy crashed through a display of them, tripped, and tumbled to the wood. A balding man in a black shirt and white apron was on his heels. Tall and lanky, he took two steps, and grabbed the boy by the nape of the neck. "Whoa, there, Davey Parker. Where do you think you're going?"

"Hey now, hold on," Dent quick-stepped up to the scene. "What's going on here?"

The man surveyed Dent top to bottom with suspicion, but he didn't miss the badge. "You the new sheriff?"

"For the time being." The little boy, who barely came to their hips, was struggling against the hold, grunting, and swinging his fists. Dent lifted the lad's chin and peered into a dirty, angry face. "What's this all about?"

"Mr. McGyver says I ate some candy. I didn't eat anything. See?" Davey Parker opened his mouth wide and stuck out his tongue. Dent leaned a little closer and had to agree; he didn't see any obvious signs of candy theft.

He straightened and tagged McGyver on the shoulder. "If he stole anything, the evidence is gone."

McGyver scowled at the boy, jerking on his collar. "If you didn't take anything, why'd you run?"

The little boy's face fell, and his fury melted away. Downcast, he whispered, " 'Cause I was thinkin' about it."

Dent and McGyver exchanged thinly-veiled looks of amusement. McGyver released the boy and smoothed his shirt. "I guess I made a mistake, Davey. My apologies."

Relief and joy lit up the boy's eyes. "You ain't gonna turn me in to the sheriff?"

"No, I guess this time we'll let things go." McGyver wagged a finger at the boy, "But give me your word you won't steal anything from me ... ever."

"I sure won't. I promise." Beaming, Davey switched to Dent, with hope burning bright. "Can I go then, Sheriff?"

Dent dropped a hand on his gun. Now he was a babysitter. This job just kept getting better and better. But he knew he couldn't dismiss the boy too easily. Like it or not, there was a lesson here that begged to be taught. "Billy the Kid started out this way, son. Stay out of trouble; don't cause your momma any grief." He leaned down a little and let a sinister tone creep into his voice. "You don't ever want me coming after you. Understand?"

The boy's eyes saucered big as dinner plates and he nodded wildly.

"Then git on home."

The boy raced off like wolves were after him.

"Well, Sheriff, maybe that's one boy you won't ever have to arrest. I sure think you threw the fear of God into him." McGyver nodded good-bye and started tidying up his brooms.

Dent wondered if it could be that easy to make a difference in someone's life. Helping a young boy avoid trouble was certainly easier than hunting a grown man down and ending his life with a bullet ... or dropping a noose over his neck.

He had the troublesome feeling maybe he'd been missing out on some of the finer aspects of this job ... and Ben had been trying to tell him exactly that.

A little bewildered by this day's complexities, he repositioned the podium on his shoulder and headed on to the sheriff's office.

"*It* ... was my ... happy lot to be ac ... ac ..."

"Accepted." Amy sat beside Israel at his desk, leaning over him as he read. He was slow, but determined, and she would reward that tenacity with patience.

He nodded and continued reading. "Accepted for adop ... adop ..."

"Adoption. Remember *tion*, t-i-o-n, makes the *shun* sound." She squeezed his shoulder and smiled. "You're doing wonderfully."

The boy's cheeks flamed and he returned to the reader, shifting in his seat. "And at the time of the kare ... kare ..."

"Ceremony. The c in this word makes the s sound."

"Ceremony." His brows knitted together, as if that made no sense whatsoever, but he continued. "Ceremony, I was reeee ... ceived?" he looked up at her for confirmation, and Amy nodded. Puffing up, he finished the sentence, "by the two squ ... squ ... squaws, to supply ... the place ... of their mother .... in the family."

Amy ruffled his hair, a show of affection normally reserved for her brother. If she could have, she would have adopted Israel. "Oh, I'm so impressed. You've improved drastically in just two weeks. You'll be reading at grade-level before Christmas," she squeezed his arm. "Maybe even above it."

"You really think so, Miss Tate?"

"I do indeed."

Unexpectedly, Israel said, "I wish my ma could have met you. She would have liked you."

Amy smiled, but inside, her heart shattered for the boy. "I'm sure I would have liked her too. I have a little brother. George is his name. You remind me so much of him ... and I miss him."

"He ain't alive no more?"

"No, he's fine, he's just back home in Ohio."

A shuffling noise at the door brought them round. Mayor Coker strolled his large, muscular frame through the door, tapped his cane on the floor, and grinned at them. "Good afternoon, Miss Tate." His smile faded. "Israel." The mayor removed his hat. "Son, I need to have a word with your teacher there. Why don't you run along?"

Amy's stomach rolled and she squeezed Israel's arm, hoping he wouldn't move. "I'm sorry, Mayor, I'm tutoring Israel, and this is the only time we have available. If I had known you were coming ..."

Mayor Coker's face darkened, but he smiled again, in spite of what he obviously thought was a lack of cooperation. "Well, I see; then, perhaps you wouldn't mind if I wait."

"Wait?" Amy prayed for some way of getting the man out of here. "I have an idea, Mayor; what about dinner?"

"Dinner?" His face brightened.

"Yes. And you could invite the members of the town council whom I haven't met yet. And any other town officials." The sheriff, of course, came to mind, but she couldn't come up with a way to suggest inviting him without sounding as if she wanted his company. But she did. Especially if she had to be around the mayor.

Mayor Coker slipped his hat on. "That's a fine idea. I'll arrange it. Let's say seven?"

CHAPTER 16

*D*ent had flirted briefly with the idea of heading out to the ranch for a cold dinner and some solitude, but Susan's cooking was just too good to pass up. The smells of stew, cornbread, and apple pie convinced him he'd made the right decision taking Doc up on the invitation. He settled at the table once more, and tried to ignore the nagging idea that he was really there to see Miss Tate. In a month of dinners together with the Woodruffs, he hadn't had much to say to her, but the feel of her pressed against him ... all warm and soft and curvaceous and smelling like roses. Well, suffice it to say he was fighting some new ideas about the schoolteacher.

But he was a man, and it was only natural to be a little attracted to the woman. She was pretty, after all. He had a handle on this, he assured himself. When the time came, he would head out of Evergreen. No backward glances, no regrets.

He scooped a heaping helping of roast onto his plate and dropped the ladle back into the pot. "You know, it's not part of my deal, Susan," he licked some broth off a knuckle. "You don't have to feed me every night. I can go to the ranch or eat at Milly's Café, but I sure do prefer your cookin'."

She dismissed him with a wave of her napkin. "I'm glad. I like having you and Amy around."

"Amy, huh? That her first name?" All this time, he'd never known her first name, never bothered to ask it. Hadn't caught it at the dinner table when Susan used it. He liked it. The name fit her. He took a bite of roast and asked casually, "Soooo, where is Miss Tate tonight? I guess she'll be eating in her cabin from now on?"

He thought he heard Doc chuckle or snort; he wasn't sure. Dent frowned at the old man. Getting the message, his friend scooped up some of the beef and lowered his head, but Dent saw the smile nonetheless.

"She's eating with the mayor tonight." Grimacing, Susan buttered a cornbread muffin.

"The mayor?" Dent heard the disapproval in his own voice and lamented it.

"She didn't want to go," Susan dipped her bread in the stew, "but it was that or meet privately with him."

"Privately?"

Doc chuckled, more openly this time. "You sound like a parrot."

Dent tightened his jaw and held his peace; at least to Doc. "How did she get there? And how is she going to get home?" he asked slowly.

Doc busted out laughing, but squashed it when he saw Dent's and Susan's dour expressions. "Hmmm. Excuse me," he tossed his napkin on the table and stood up. "Believe I'll get that pitcher of buttermilk from the kitchen."

His shoulders shook as he left the table. Doc's good humor was not contagious, and Dent intended to talk to the old man about it.

"Henry dropped her off, but I was hoping you'd fetch her."

He swung back to Susan. "This isn't New York City, and I'm not a cab."

"You took her home last night. What makes tonight different? Just because she's at the mayor's?" She waved an accusing spoon at him. "Can you honestly say you have something more important to do than escort a lady home?"

...In the dark, of which she's terrified, and out of the clutches of a scoundrel? Dent sagged, chastised by Susan's question. "Reckon I've got time."

"Good." Relieved, Susan dipped her spoon, then lifted it to her lips and blew off the steam. "I thought you might get into a habit. Of walking her home, that is."

"I don't know about a habit, but I sometimes start my rounds at that end of town."

Doc guffawed from the kitchen. Susan quickly took the bite of her soup. Dent didn't miss the joke and at whose expense. He squeezed the spoon so tightly in his hand, he could feel it bending. "Doc, if you've got something to say, I wish you'd just say it and quit all this snickerin' and gigglin'."

"All right, fine," the old man yelled, bursting into the dining room, carrying his pitcher of buttermilk. "I'm tired of seeing your sorry face at my table every night. Why don't you eat at Milly's Café tomorrow night and take Miss Tate with you?"

Dent's mouth literally fell open. "Why would I do that?"

This time, Susan joined in the laughter with her husband.

Dent mounted Ginger, his broad-chested sorrel, and trotted the two blocks to the mayor's house ... stewing the whole way. He did not like being the butt of Doc's jokes. If he hadn't known the Woodruffs his whole life, he would have given them some strongly-worded reminders about staying out of his business.

Maybe Miss Tate was a *bit* of a distraction. That was all. She'd grown on him some, but not in any way that mattered a wit to his plans. He realized it had barely been a month, but he could feel Evergreen trying to draw him back home. Or maybe it wasn't the town.

It doesn't matter. I'm not staying.

Pa's killers were still out there, and he finally had some legitimate clues to follow.

He pounded on the door, rattling it on its hinges. Embarrassed by his heavy hand, he faded off. Momentarily, a gray-haired, round-faced black woman opened the door and grinned at Dent, bright white teeth glowing against her ebony skin. "Why, Mister Hernandez, what a pleasant surprise."

Dent jerked his hat off and grinned at the old woman. "Matilda. It's been a long time."

"Too long," she slapped him on his shoulder, "Good to see you, son. Come on in."

Dent had never been inside the mayor's mansion, but he'd heard whispers about the opulence of it. He surveyed the lavishly-furnished, antebellum-style home, and whistled. Light from the massive chandelier overhead sparkled and glimmered, casting an almost hypnotic light on the grand foyer. The rumors were true. Persian rugs covered the intricate, inlaid wood floors. Fine paintings and animal trophies adorned the walls. Exquisite furniture filled the rooms.

Matilda followed his appraisal of the home and nodded. "Yep, Mayor Coker don't do nothin' on a small scale."

"I can see that."

"Well, let me fetch him for ya."

"No ma'am," he answered too fast, twirling his hat in his hands, but the last person he wanted to see was the mayor.

This house, his extravagant wealth, bothered him. "No, I mean, I'm here to pick up Miss Tate. She requested an escort home."

Matilda smiled knowingly. "Smart girl. I'll let her know you're here."

The housekeeper shuffled down the hall, and Dent again took in the stunning decadence of the abode. Evergreen had been good to the man. Too good. He had to wonder at the amazing fortune.

"Sheriff," Mayor Coker called gaily, swaying slightly as he strode down the hall, half-empty liquor glass in hand. "What a pleasant surprise. What can I do for you?"

Matilda apologized with a shake of her head and disappeared through a door. Dent steeled himself against the annoying man and smiled. "Mayor, I came for Miss Tate."

Coker grabbed Dent's shoulder and breathed whiskey in his face. "You want her, do you?" He wiggled his eyebrows and leaned in conspiratorially. "So do I, and, being the mining expert that I am, I'm quite sure I'm the man to plumb those depths—"

Dent smacked the man's hand away. "You need to hobble that mouth of yours ... *Mayor*."

Coker's jaw clenched. "Your suggestion, though dazzling in its candor, has no bearing on my point." He leaned in, swaying a little, and again clutched Dent's shoulder. "Perhaps I can grease the wheels with that judge and get you out of here a little faster. I mean to have Miss Tate and I mean for you to get out of the way."

The comments blindsided Dent. He had no idea why the mayor was running off at the mouth like this, or speaking so crudely of Miss Tate. He suspected the man couldn't hold his whiskey. But reasons didn't matter at the moment. "Coker, you're the mayor of this town, but if you say one more ungentlemanly thing about Miss Tate—" he went almost nose-to-nose with the man, "I will arrest you for public drunkenness."

Coker's face darkened and he drew back. "You can't arrest me for that in my own home."

"Who said you'd be in your home?" The two men stared at each other, engaged in a war of wills. "And I'll tell you something else. Lay your hand on me again, and you will meet with an accident—*in your own home.*"

The mayor licked his lips and inched back. "Just like your father. He didn't know when to back down either."

Dent straightened. "What do you mean by that?"

Coker waved his glass. "I know the story. He and Ben were outgunned and outnumbered, but they fought anyway. A smart man knows when he's licked, Dent. I thought you were smart."

"What are you talking about?" Dent asked carefully. He had the disorienting feeling he'd walked into a conversation with the mayor that had been going on for a long time already.

Suddenly Coker's icy demeanor thawed and he grinned charmingly, just as easily as the wind changing direction. "Dent, this isn't how I want things between us. For the time that you're here, we have to work together. I know you can't get out of Evergreen fast enough. Stay away from Miss Tate, sell me your ranch, and I'll do everything I can to see that you leave quickly ... and smoothly."

Dent dropped a hand to his hip and cocked his head to one side. "I have no idea why we're talking about Miss Tate. What's more, I have no idea why you'd think I'd sell you Ben's ranch."

Coker smiled again, but it melted into an indolent sneer. "I got your Pa's ranch. I'll get Ben's."

Dent tried to absorb what felt like a kick to his guts. "What do you mean, you've got Pa's ranch?"

Coker staggered back a step and waved his hand dismissively. "I bought it from that fool you sold it to. Kilkenny ran that place into the ground in less than a year."

"You going into ranching?" Pa's spread wasn't big enough for a real, money-making operation, not like the kind this tinhorn would want. Combining it with Ben's might make it more attractive, but there were other, bigger ranches around.

Before Coker could answer, Dent heard the swish of a skirt. Hands folded demurely at her waist, Miss Tate approached the battlefield hesitantly. "Gentlemen?" Coker wheeled around. "Mayor, thank you for a lovely evening, and for the introductions, but I'll be leaving now."

CHAPTER 17

The shadows of trees along the empty street swayed eerily with the chilly fall breeze. Amy pulled her wool coat a little tighter, but for warmth, not because she was afraid. Well, she was ... a little. While this particular trek was new to her, all the neighborhoods she'd seen in Evergreen were as pretty as a Currier and Ives card, mysterious shadows notwithstanding. And the man beside her engendered an undeniable feeling of security.

She risked a quick peek at the lawman. Sheriff Hernandez, his horse in tow, fairly stalked and stewed as they ambled toward her cottage. His brooding expression, difficult to discern in the darkness beneath the brim of his hat, was clear enough from his hunched shoulders and heavy steps. She assumed his dark mood had more to do with the mayor than her ... but what if it didn't? What if he didn't like being a nanny? The man had walked her home last night, checked to make sure the cabin was safely empty, and walked the grounds before departing. *Lord, he did everything but tuck me in bed.*

Perhaps he found the duty as demeaning as participating in the pumpkin carving contest.

Convincing herself that she was more the cause of his mood than Mayor Coker, Amy determined to release the sheriff. And the Woodruffs as well, who escorted her everywhere when the sheriff wasn't available. She had to get past her ridiculous fears. "Sheriff Hernandez, I've been thinking. I'm such a burden on your time—"

"You're no burden, ma'am," he said, with all the enthusiasm of a man off to visit the dentist.

She deflated. "Well, that's kind of you to say, but I'm a grown woman and I'm dealing with my fears. You needn't ... occupy yourself with me."

His head jerked up. "I take it you would prefer to have the mayor escort you home?"

"What?" she choked out, stopping abruptly and rounding on him. "Oh, good grief, no. You misunderstand me, Sheriff. Perhaps I shouldn't say it, but, frankly, I find the mayor boorish and overbearing." She thought she saw a slight relaxation of his shoulders then, and his chin lifted. Something seemed to hang in the air between them, but, in the darkness, she could not read his face to make any guesses. Pushing past the awkward moment, she resumed walking. "I do think his wife, May Beth, is lovely, though." Then the deeper implication of his statement hit her. Angry, she snagged his arm and they both stopped again. "Wait just a moment. What do you mean by assuming I would want that oaf to walk me home? He's a married man. What kind of a woman do you think *I am*?" Her voice rose with her anger as she took a step toward him, wagging a finger in his face. "Clearly, I don't need to ask, if that is your assumption."

"Ma'am ... Miss Tate," he stepped back from her and raised his hand, "I did not mean to insinuate ... I only meant ... that is ..."

Amy doubted he could see her face in this darkness, but he could see her hands on her hips, a rapidly tapping toe, and her chest rising and falling like she'd run a mile. He couldn't be so dense as to not understand how deeply he'd offended her. "You only meant *what?*"

"Well, he has a reputation with women, I hear. Those pearly white teeth of his and that big mansion—"

"I am not a ... a prostitute, Sheriff Hernandez."

She did see the whites of his eyes then, as they nearly bugged out of his head and he snatched his hat off his head. "Miss Tate, I deeply regret that you think that I was insinuating anything like that. I would never ..."

Stomping her foot, Amy growled at the man and charged off into the darkness. "You are your own comedy of errors, Sheriff."

---

*D*ent stood there for a moment, staring up at the starry sky. Rolling his hat around in his hands, he wished the early October breeze would blow away his embarrassment. He caught a whiff of her magical perfume and hung his head. He didn't figure a thing he could say was going to fix this blunder, but he couldn't call himself any kind of a man if he didn't at least offer a full-throated apology.

He rushed to catch up with her, and matched her gait. "Miss Tate, I am not the most eloquent man. You could argue I'm about as gifted at talking to a woman as a chicken is to flying, but," he raised his voice and spoke firmly, "I did not mean to imply anything untoward about your character or reputation. I am truly sorry for the offense I've caused."

Dent stopped. Miss Tate took several more steps before she finally slowed down then stopped as well. Slowly, she turned back to him. She cocked her head to one side and he heard her huff a frustrated breath. He drummed his fingers on his leg, sure she was waiting for him to say more. Fine. Eat a little crow. He'd insulted the woman; pretty badly, actually.

"If you are not interested in the mayor's company, Miss Tate, it would be my pleasure to walk you home." Her continued stubborn silence both annoyed and worried him. "It's no burden. *You* are no burden." Oh, hang it all, he thought. She was a woman, and she needed some pretty words to soothe that ego. "Miss Tate, would you … accept my apology over dinner one night? I mean, would you allow me to escort you to a real restaurant?" His mouth nearly fell open at the request. It had leaped forth from his mouth almost as if, somehow, his brain had bypassed his will.

But her shoulders softened and the rod went out of her back. Feeling it was safe to approach her, he ambled closer, close enough to see the slight smile on her face as she asked, "A real restaurant?"

Dent's relief at the truce surprised him. Unable to back out, wondering if he would even if he could, he shrugged a shoulder. "Yes ma'am. Milly's. Maybe tomorrow ni—" He shook his head. *Cheyenne.* "I'm sorry, maybe Saturday? I've got to go to Cheyenne for a couple of days."

"Cheyenne again?" she touched her lips, "Oh, that is none of my business."

"Just some legal work." He shook his head, disinclined to mention the reason for his presence at another hanging. "But I should be back late Thursday night. Would *Friday* evening be agreeable?"

For a moment, he thought she might say no. "Yes, Sheriff, that would be agreeable."

They both started walking again. "You could call me 'Dent', if you wanted to." He realized he was twirling his hat around like a fidgety twelve-year-old and dropped it on his head. He frowned at his awkward conversation. Why couldn't he talk to Miss Tate the way he talked to Maddie, over in Lander? Like he didn't ...

Care.

"You could call me 'Amy', if you like." Her voice trembled a little at the end, as if she was nervous.

He rolled the name around again in his head. *Amy.* But something told him if he said it back to her, he'd be crossing a line into unexplored country. Before he could decide, the clip-clop of hooves intruded. He squinted down the street at the approaching rider. In the dark, he couldn't be sure ...

"Dent?" a woman's voice called.

Susan? "Susan, what is it?"

The woman kicked her horse and covered the last several yards between them at a canter. "It's Israel." She reined up. "Tom beat the hound out of him. Doc's tending to him. He said he thought you'd want to know."

Miss Tate clutched her throat. "Is Israel all right?"

"He got away before Tom could kill him, but he's in rough shape."

Dent spun on his horse, clutched the saddle horn, and swung up, his gaze locked on Susan. "Where's the Packett place?"

"Eddie Stewart's old homestead."

He shifted his attention to Amy. "You go on with Susan. I'm gonna pay Tom Packett a visit."

CHAPTER 18

*D*ent raced across town and out to the fringes. A full moon lit his way, the frost sparkling like scattered diamonds on the undulating hills and eerie rock formations. The cold air stung his face, threatening to numb his hands. He flexed his fingers on the reins and spurred Ginger for a little more speed.

Dent felt bad for Israel, but he couldn't deny the anticipation quickening his heart. Finally, a little trouble in this podunk town. He would enjoy a friendly *visit* with a man who beat children. Maybe, if he was lucky, Tom Packett would do something stupid.

A light glowed in the distance, and Dent took the next road on his right, slowing Ginger down gradually. He crested the hill and peered down on a one-room cabin, light coming from the front window. Dent pulled the horse to a stop and surveyed the homestead bathed in silvery moonlight. Fences sat in disarray, posts and rails leaning in all directions. The door to the barn hung askew. The porch on the house sagged. Weeds grew around the house, in the garden, and choked a dilapidated chicken coop.

He eased Ginger up to the front of the house, listening for a moment. Silence. "Hello in the house!" Not getting an immediate response, he tried again. "Hello in the house! This is Sheriff Hernandez! If you're in there, Tom Packett, you'd best answer me!"

After a moment, a scuffling sound reached him, then he heard the latch on the door, and a man stepped out on to the porch. Though silhouetted in the weak light, Dent had no trouble making out the shotgun draped in his arms.

"Somethin' I can do for you, *Sheriff Hernandez?*"

Dent had heard that tone of voice a million times. Arrogant, contemptuous. A man who hated the law, despised authority.

Dent's favorite kind of outlaw.

He almost grinned. "Your son is at Doc Woodruff's, getting patched up. He pulls through, I'm gonna convince him to press charges against you for assault and battery."

Packett snorted. "Lawdogs. You're all the same. Think everything is your business."

"When a citizen of Evergreen gets attacked, beat to within an inch of his life, you can bet I will make that my business, yes, sir."

"He's my son. You can't come on my property and tell me how to raise him."

Dent raised his finger. "It just so happens I have an eviction notice on my desk." He grinned at the cheer in his own voice. "I have been dragging my feet about serving it." He leaned forward, the leather of the saddle squeaking its protest. "I will be back tomorrow with the notice, at which time, I will escort you off these *lovely* premises."

"There's only one way you'll take me outta here, lawdog."

Dent chuckled, a cold, deadly sound. "Promise?"

A dying outlaw had once told Dent *I heard the sound of death in your voice. I knew I should have run.* Packett should run. Some of the man's bravado seemed to seep away, as if he were contemplating that very idea. The shotgun lowered a bit, his shoulders drooping a smidgen.

"You the Hernandez that used to be a U.S. Marshal?"

Dent smiled at the fear he heard. "Still am." Most outlaws, given their choice, did not want to face him. He had earned his reputation for just as willingly bringing in a man dead as alive. Outlaws knew the possible outcome if they wanted to tangle with him. "Expect me around seven in the morning."

He backed Ginger up a good twenty yards before he swung her around and headed back up the hill. On the ridge, he stole a quick glance back. The man still stood in the doorway, as if frozen to the spot.

Apparently he thawed. When Dent stopped by the next morning, Tom Packett was gone.

---

*A*my peeked through the examination room's door. Israel lay on the bed, sleeping soundly. She was relieved to see that the swelling had already started going down in his lip, but it was still a terrible shade of purple and twice its normal size. His nose, puffy and sporting a nice cut on the bridge, at least wasn't crooked. Last night, his appearance had ripped a sob from her; his blood had been everywhere.

Now, in the light of day and cleaned up, Israel had fared much better than she at first thought.

"He'll be up and around in a day or two," Doc whispered from behind her. "No broken ribs, no internal bleeding, his nose isn't even broken. Guess his pa was too drunk to hit him very hard."

With that, Doc drifted away, and Amy sighed. She so wanted to help Israel, but couldn't do anything at the moment. Well, she could keep him company, perhaps, be there when he woke up. Clutching a batch of spelling tests, she slipped into the boy's room and settled in the chair next to his bed. Quietly, she began grading the quizzes.

Her mind kept wandering, though. Dent had come by the doctor's office last night to let them know he would attempt to evict Packett, but he never answered the question of where Israel might wind up. Without a home, what was the boy supposed to do, where was he supposed to live?

Concerned for him, she reached out and gently pressed the back of her hand to his forehead. *Good. No fever.* He woke at her touch, and she jerked her hand away. "I'm sorry. I didn't mean to wake you."

He regarded the spelling tests in her lap and raised an eyebrow. "You come to tutor me some more?" he asked weakly, a half-smile moving his swollen lip.

"Well," she tapped on the papers, embarrassed she'd been so zealous. "I do have the reader with me, if you're up to it."

Israel closed his eyes. "Maybe, in a bit. I'm doin' good, ain't I? I mean, aren't I?"

Amy bit her lip and blinked back tears. "Yes, Israel, you are doing very well. You sleep now. I'll be here when you wake up."

Again, his lips moved a little, indicating a smile. "Good."

She watched him for a moment, charmed by his soft, smooth cheeks. He had a handsome face that was beginning to sharpen with adulthood. Israel Packet was becoming a man, and a man should know how to read so he could make his way in the world. Amy promised she would do her best to give him that chance. A chance to excel, a chance to succeed ... a chance to get away from his black-hearted father.

She moved to the next test to grade. Israel's. His first since they'd started their lessons together. Her heart beating a little faster, she graded it and, with each correct answer, her pulse raced even faster. He'd gotten all twenty words right! She checked the extra credit word, and let a happy tear slide down her cheek. Israel Packett had spelled *elocution* correctly.

God, help me to truly make a difference in this boy's life. He's already made a difference in mine.

The perfect spelling grade on Israel's test had lit a fire in the boy, and Amy rejoiced for him. His new-found confidence was reflected in his reading skills. To help him pass the time at Doc's she'd spent three whole afternoons with him, rather than the mere hour of tutoring. Five minutes here at his bedside today, listening to him read from his primer, she knew he was ready for a more difficult book.

"Oh, I am so pleased at your progress, Israel. Another month or so, and you'll be reading at grade-level, I'm sure of it."

His chest puffed up and pride lifted his countenance. "You really think so, Miss Tate?"

"Oh, I know so." Now, if she only knew where the boy was going to wind up staying. The front door opened and she heard the shuffle of boots. She rose to her feet. "Let me see who that is. Doc's on a call."

She reached for the door, but it burst open. Amy squeaked and stepped back.

A tall man, dirty hair hanging in greasy strings, and hate burning in his dark eyes, loomed over the room. "Get dressed, boy. We're going home."

Amy watched helplessly as Israel obediently tossed the covers back. She couldn't let him go, but her heart caught in her throat, and her pulse hammered wildly. Israel reached for his breeches draped across the foot of the bed.

No, no, no. Amy found her voice and her courage. "Mr.

Packett, I presume? Doc hasn't released Israel. You can't take him with you yet. He's still recovering from—" *you*, she almost said, but caught herself. "From the accident. And I thought you'd been evicted. Where will you take him?"

Packett straightened up, bushy eyebrows rising. "You the boy's teacher?"

"Yes sir, and he's doing quite well. I'm really very pleas—"

"So how come you to know about the sheriff threatening to evict me?"

"Uh ... uh," for a moment, her words tripped over her tongue, a creeping fear trying to steal her wits. She had to stay calm and polite, though the man terrified her. "The sheriff stopped by the night we brought Israel in and said he was going to evict you. We've been searching for a place for Israel to stay."

"Well, he don't need it now. My mortgage is paid in full, and there ain't a dang thing the sheriff or anybody else can do about it. Hurry up and get your pants on, Israel."

"Where'd you get the money for that, Pa?" Israel sounded stunned.

Packett's face reddened and his jaw clenched. "I don't reckon that's yours or anybody else's business."

Despairing, Amy silently implored Israel. The boy nodded calmly as he slipped his pants on over his long johns. "It's all right, Miss Tate. I was ready to get out of that bed anyway."

Oh, where is Dent? she wondered miserably. He could stop this and keep Israel here and safe. She wiped a sweaty palm on her dress and squeezed Israel's shoulder. "All right then. I'll see you in school tomorrow."

CHAPTER 19

Maddie brought Dent a whiskey and sat down across the table from him. She was a pretty woman, with golden hair piled high in a messy, casual sort of way. She ran this saloon and the boardinghouse next door, both of which produced a decent profit, though The Lost Souls was empty at the moment. She had told him often she was waiting for him to ask her to run away with him, promising they would go in style because of all the money she'd saved.

Frowning, he tapped his index finger on the shot glass. Problem was, now he wasn't sure where he wanted to go, if he wanted to go anywhere at all. He just had this itchy feeling he didn't want to be here. Then where – ?

"Hanging go all right today?" Maddie asked.

"Uhmm."

He heard her sigh and forced his attention back to her. "What?"

"How many years have you been coming to see me, Dent?"

He shrugged, wondering what that had to do with anything. "I dunno. A few anyway."

"Four. Four years you've been riding through here when the whim hit, or when you needed healing from a hanging. Today is the first time I'm not sure you're here because you love me."

The word touched a nerve, accusing him of promises that had never passed his lips. "I've never said I love you."

"You never said you didn't. And you've let me talk and talk about all the places we can go when I sell out. I can afford to start us over together anywhere in the world." She leaned back in her chair, her shoulders sagging. "Whenever you'd come here, I'd feel at least ... *affection*." Her voice softened. "But not now. Why?"

A simple enough question ... one he couldn't answer. And why the devil did Amy Tate's face with her silly, silver spectacles rise up in his mind?

Maddie reached over and grabbed Dent's empty glass, poured herself a shot, and tossed it back. Eyes shut for a moment, she bore the burn, then smiled sadly at him. "I guess I knew all along you were just using me."

"I sort of thought we were using each other."

Her face went slack, but then quickly contorted into a flinty expression, one that said she'd like to cut out his heart.

"To be honest, Maddie, I don't know what's wrong with me." He tapped his fingers for a minute on the green felt then grabbed his hat. "But I'm gonna be riding on." He didn't say it harshly. "I'm not much for company tonight."

She rose with him and wrapped her knuckles twice on the table. "You just came by to cut the ties. I guess that's better than leaving me wonderin'. Thank you."

Dent heard the unspoken good-bye, and he agreed. He hadn't consciously planned this, but he knew he wouldn't be back. He supposed he could wonder about deeper meanings here, the reason for this farewell, and where his feet wanted to lead him, but he preferred not to think about anything at all.

By Friday morning, Amy was full of butterflies. She was eager to see Israel and let him read aloud in class. She couldn't deny, though, that some of those butterflies were all aflutter over dinner with a handsome sheriff.

She set her pencil down on her planning book and rose to stoke the fire. The classroom was fighting to hang on to the October morning's chill. At least none of the students had arrived yet. She felt it was her duty to have the room warm, tidy, and inviting, to show them she cared.

Shortly, the class filled up with her children, and the morning progressed. As the hours passed, though, her heart grew heavier with worry. Israel wasn't merely tardy, he wasn't coming at all. Oh, that father of his. She wanted to strangle the man. By the end of the day, she'd determined to visit the Packetts' place. If Susan wouldn't take her, she'd walk. The idea made her mouth go dry.

For God hath not given us the spirit of fear, but of power, and love, and of a sound mind.

Oh, Father, I've got to claim that. I've got to believe that ... I've got to trust You that I will be all right. There is not danger behind every tree and bush. And I have to make sure Israel is all right.

Resolve like a metal rod straightened her spine and she marched around the room, gathering text books, sweeping away chalk dust, and collecting forgotten gloves and scarves. The jingle of Susan's wagon announced Amy's ride, and she hurried to deposit the clothing on her desk. Praying Susan would go with her to the Packetts', she rushed to the alcove at the front of the school to get her coat.

As she slid into her lovely, red wool dolman, a recent gift from her parents, Dent pushed open the door and peeked inside the schoolhouse. His eyes, the warm color of fresh coffee, glittered with cheer. "All right if I come in?"

"Of course." A fresh flutter of butterflies took flight in her stomach and temporarily suppressed her burdensome concern for Israel. "I thought you were Susan." He was ruggedly handsome in the thick sheepskin coat. It gave his tanned skin a healthy glow. Then she noticed he'd shaved. Even his dungarees appeared pressed.

Dent whipped his hat from his head and shrugged, but through the coat, she could barely tell it. "I was hoping you might be interested in an early dinner."

Israel. "Honestly, I would like that, but there was something I'd planned to do right after school."

"Oh, well, uh, could I give you a ride somewhere then?"

Amy grinned, silently thanking God for the escort. There was no one she could be safer with. "That would be a blessing. It's not a call I was eager to make alone." She finished her last button and raised her head, hoping her determination was evident. "But I *was* going to make it."

His brow rose. "Must be important."

"I was going out to see Israel Packett."

"Israel? Where's he at?"

"Tom Packett stopped by Doc's office yesterday, and practically forced Israel to go with him. He said he'd paid the mortgage in full, so they went home."

Dent's face darkened and he rubbed his chin. "Now, where did he get money for that?"

"Israel asked the same question." She pulled her gloves from her pocket and started working into them. "Anyway, I'm worried. He didn't come to school today."

Dent motioned toward the door. "Why don't we go see if we can find out what's going on?"

Dent would be the first to admit that, once he smelled trouble, he could be pretty single-minded about ferreting it out. Amy, however, sitting so close to him on the wagon seat they could rub elbows, had a persistent way of interrupting his thoughts.

The sun was sinking fast behind the low hills of Fremont County, throwing the rock formations and pine forests into long, dark shadows. The breeze had a bite to it, too, promising more than frost on the pumpkin. "Colder than you thought?" he asked as she hunched her shoulders.

She pushed her spectacles up on her nose and shook her head. "No, no, I'm fine, Sheriff."

He should have his mind on Packett and where that money came from, but hearing her say *Sheriff* after their last conversation about names bothered him. He'd been rolling *Amy* around in his head ever since he'd left Maddie. Funny, he'd never had any trouble saying *her* name.

"Do you suspect, perhaps, Mr. Packett stole the money?" she asked.

"I find it mighty strange he's erratic on his loan payments for months and months and now, all of a sudden, he pays off the whole note. I'll send some telegrams out, see if there's been trouble anywhere around. Robberies and the like."

Of course, he supposed Packett could have taken a train somewhere, committed a robbery, then come back. Or maybe, he simply sold something. But he would have to know paying off the mortgage would make some folks suspicious. Dent had a sense about men, and Tom Packett was a tough customer. He was capable of all sorts of meanness ... and Amy had thought about coming out here alone.

He stole a sideways peek at her. She had a kind of cute up-turned nose, and a rosy flush to her cheeks from the cold.

Hair the color of melted caramel swirled gently around her shoulders. "Coming out here to check on Israel was pretty ..." He almost said *stupid*. And it was, but it was also something else. "Brave. Not the best idea, but brave. You're getting ...?" he faded off, not sure how to ask.

"Getting better? Braver?" She traced the flowers in her dress. "I think so. I love my students. They are so full of energy and innocence. I don't know how to explain it, but they bring me peace."

He studied her more directly and nodded. "I can see that." She met his gaze and they both half-smiled at each other. "About calling you ... 'Amy'; is that offer still good?"

Her smile transformed to a wide, welcoming grin. "Absolutely."

CHAPTER 20

Amy's pleasure at Dent saying her first name pleased him as they rode the last two miles to Packett's place ... and vexed him. *It's just a name ...*

Yet, he liked saying it. She liked hearing it.

As they topped the hill overlooking the small ranch, he reminded himself sternly to focus on things at hand. Smoke poured from a mud-and-twig chimney, and, in the twilight, an amber light glowed from one window. The horse's hooves and jangling harness announced their arrival, and Dent made no attempt to quiet either. Before he could pull the rig to a halt, Packett appeared on the porch, again holding the shotgun.

"What are you doing here, lawdog?"

Dent clenched his jaw, determined not to let this scum goad him into a fight, not yet. "We came to check on Israel. Miss Tate here said he wasn't in school today."

"He's done with that foolishness. I need him around here to fix up the place."

"Yeah, speaking of ..." Dent scanned the house and yard. Something was different about the ranch, but he couldn't put his finger on it. "I heard you paid off your mortgage. Where'd you get the money? You steal it?"

A slow sneer lifted the man's lip. "No, I didn't. Israel," he called over his shoulder. "Come out here, boy."

Dishes clattered inside then Israel stepped outside and stood beside his father. His attention riveted on Amy. "Evening, Miss Tate."

"Israel, I missed you in school today."

"Well, I—" the boy shifted uneasily.

Packett motioned with the shotgun. "Tell these fine folks," his voice dripped with sarcasm, "I did not steal the money to pay off our mortgage."

"N-no," Israel stammered, "Pa didn't steal it. That's the truth, Sheriff Hernandez."

Dent sagged a little. He didn't like Tom Packett. Not one ounce. Israel was covering for him, too, but he wasn't sure how exactly. Something just felt wrong here, but that didn't change the fact there was nothing Dent could do. "Israel, your pa can't beat you like he did. You could press charges."

Israel took a step forward. "No sir, I can't do that." He shook his head. "I mean, I won't do that."

Dent refrained from sighing, but it took effort. He'd known the answer before he'd asked it.

"Israel, I hope to see you in school Monday. Your reading was progressing so w—"

"I said he's done with that foolishness." Tom Packet stomped to the edge of his porch. "Now, get off my land and don't come back."

"Please, Miss Tate. Leave," the boy implored her with a tense expression.

Amy sighed and leaned back, admitting defeat?

Dent studied the yard and ramshackle home one more time, unable to pin down what bothered him exactly. "We'll leave. But men like you always give the law a reason to come back. Lay another hand on that boy, and I'll be out here faster than you can blink." He raised the reins, ready to snap them. "And I'll find something to arrest you for."

The buckboard rumbled and bounced its way down the dirt road as twilight slowly died to full dark. A handful of lights glittered in the distance, letting Amy know the town wasn't too far away. The empty expanse of rolling hills and treeless plains could have frightened her, perhaps would have under different circumstances, but her heart was too full of pain for Israel.

She was upset about the boy's situation, but she couldn't help being impressed by Dent's promise to deal with Packett if he touched his son again.

"I guess that was no way to start an evening out with a pretty lady."

Amy wiggled her fingers, the cold sinking in from sitting still too long. "Actually, Dent," she smiled at the way his name rolled off her tongue, "I was thinking about how you tried to help Israel."

Dent heaved a great sigh and shook his head. "But he won't let me help him. And he won't help himself. That father of his is going to drag him down with him."

"He was coming to class every day, and I was tutoring him. He was doing so well. He wants more out of life than his current prospects offer."

"That may be true, but he's got to *keep* making good choices. If he really wants a better life, Amy, he has to get out from under his pa ... and stay away from people like him."

Amy cut into a huge chicken pot pie dripping with steaming broth that ran quickly off the ladle. "Oh, hurry, give me your plate." Dent obliged and she served him a heaping helping of Milly's Friday night special.

"Mmmm," he hummed, inhaling. "That sure smells good."

Amy filled her own plate then bowed her head and said a quick blessing. When she opened her eyes, she discovered Dent staring at her. "What?"

He reached for his fork and acted nonchalant. "I was thinking what a shame Israel didn't have a ma like you."

The statement stunned Amy, and she felt the blush spread over her cheeks. "You don't even know me that well."

"I have a good sense of people." He stabbed a piece of chicken and swirled it in the golden sauce. "Some bring good things into the world, most don't. If I asked you what's your favorite thing in the world, you'd probably say ...?"

"Books."

"And Tom Packett would probably say something like a fast horse and a faster woman—oh, that was crass. My apologies." Crimson colored his cheeks. "Doc was right. I'm pretty out of practice at making polite conversation."

"Then we'll practice."

She grinned at him, and, after a moment of debate, he returned it. "All right."

"Then tell me, what is your favorite thing in the world?"

The humor faded from his face and his attention drifted.

"I'm sorry," she said quietly. "Obviously, I said something wrong."

"No," he waved his fork at her, went back to his pie. "Memories. Memories are my favorite thing. Fishing with my pa, my ma's last birthday before she passed."

"I can't imagine how difficult it must have been, losing your parents, especially so close together ..."

He stared at his coffee cup for a moment before reaching for it. "Losing Ma because of a snake bite, that was one thing. Snakes bite. They're not evil. They don't seek you out and try to take your life and your property. The men who shot my father, on the other hand, have to face justice, and I'll find 'em ... or die trying."

Amy licked her lips, wondering if she should push this, but she could see it in his eyes what Susan feared. Dent was losing himself to hate. "Dent," she said softly, "do you think that's what your parents would want? Avenging your father's death won't bring him back."

His fork slowed, but then picked up speed again. "Maybe not, but I can make a difference in this world with a badge. I like being a lawman."

She discovered something encouraging in his words. "Because you want to help people? Like Israel."

He set his fork down and wiped his mouth, but kept the napkin scrunched in his hand. "It's been said I'm too quick to pull a trigger. The way I see it, I've had the good fortune to be the last man standing when some bad men made some bad decisions." He took a sip of coffee. "I want to find the men who killed my pa. And if some low-lifes meet justice in the process ..." He shrugged. "That's not very noble, I suppose, but it's the truth."

"What if you never find the men who killed your father?"

Before he could answer, Jim and Sarah Harper, two of her students' parents, strolled by, but stopped when they saw her. "Oh, Miss Tate," Sarah touched Amy on the shoulder, "we wanted to thank you for the note about Lydia's issues. We've had her eyes checked, and she does need glasses. Thank you."

"Well, I'm so glad you addressed my concerns and we have a solution now."

"Sheriff," Jim stuck his hand out to Dent. "Jim Harper. My wife, Sarah. Thank you for joining us here in Evergreen."

"Oh," Dent wiped his hand on his napkin and accepted the shake. "Uh, thank you for having me."

"We will miss Ben greatly, but a feisty new sheriff like you will certainly keep the riff-raff out of town." Jim winked, as if the plan was foolproof.

"Yes, the riff-raff."

Tension around his mouth made Amy think poor Dent wanted to crawl under the table.

"Well, I'll do my best," he promised the Harpers with, she guessed, strained enthusiasm.

Sarah clutched Jim's arm, pushing him onward. "Have a lovely evening then, you two." Her husband nodded good-bye and moved on.

Amy fiddled with her glasses to hide a smile. "Not used to that?"

"To what?"

"A simple thank-you."

"No, I usually hear cursing and screaming."

Amy chuckled softly, but remembered her question. "So, *have* you thought about the possibility you might never find your father's killers?"

Dent tapped his index finger on the edge of his plate. "I will. I have to."

"Then what? Will you stay a lawman?"

He thought a long moment before answering. "The fact that I am not afraid to pull a trigger makes me a better lawman than a lot of the officers out there. We live in a dark world, Amy, where most men have evil intentions. I reckon I'll keep huntin' 'em. Like I said, I'm good at it."

We do live in a dark world, and he can't see any light, Lord. He needs to see Your light. He needs ... She couldn't quite think of the word. Then it hit her. *Innocence. He needs something in his life that is still brimming with hope and promise, Father.*

It occurred to her that she might have just the right thing.

CHAPTER 21

Dent removed his hat, and slipped into an empty desk at the back of Amy's classroom. How had she talked him into this?

Their eyes met over numerous bobbing heads and waving hands and she smiled. "Class, I have a special treat for you today. We have been discussing government. How the government represents us. The people who work in the government work for *we the people*. I'd like you to meet one of your employees." She motioned for Dent to come forward. He stood, and the room was filled with gasps and squeals as the children watched him. "Meet U.S. Marshal, Dent Hernandez."

Dent started forward, amazed how he could *feel* the twenty or so eager children eying him, studying the .45 on his hip.

"We call him *Sheriff* Hernandez for now because he's working for Evergreen until we have a replacement for Sheriff Hayes."

Dent marched up and stood beside Amy, ducking his chin at the class. "Howdy."

"What do we say?" she asked.

All the children wriggled out of their seats and stood beside their desks to speak in unison, "Good Morning, Sheriff Hernandez."

"All right, class, take your seats." Amy stepped a few feet away from Dent to give him the stage. "Why don't we start with questions? Is that all right with you, Sheriff?"

The hands flew up like rockets, and Dent had to chuckle. "Sure." He pointed at a little girl with bright red hair and thick spectacles, sitting in the front row. "You."

"How long have you been a U.S. Marshal?"

"For eight years."

Then a barrage of voices unleashed, tumbling over one another. "Have you ever been shot?" "How many times?" "Have you ever been stabbed?" "How many times?" "Can we see your gun?"

Dent skillfully calmed the class and answered each question with patience and humor. The more he talked, the closer the children leaned in, enthralled with his stories. Amy sat down at her desk and hid a smile behind her hand.

"Who's the biggest outlaw you ever brung in?"

"Brought," Amy corrected.

"Frank Darnell and his gang?"

"How'd you catch 'em?"

The back-and-forth went on and on, until, Manuel Lopez raised his hand and asked, "How many men have you killed?"

The glow left Dent's face. He pulled back from the class a little. Amy leaped to her feet. "I think that is enough questions for now, don't you think, Sheriff? We've certainly kept you long enough. I'm sure there are some ruffians in town who need arresting." The class giggled.

"Not in Evergreen," Manuel muttered.

"Well, it's been my pleasure," he said to the class then he

winked at Amy. "And thank you, Miss Tate. I did enjoy this." He sounded pleasantly surprised.

---

*D*ent grabbed his coat from the hook and slipped it on outside. Standing on the school's stoop, he breathed in the scent of pines blanketing the quiet, peaceful, nearly crime-free haven of Evergreen ... the town in which he had just spent an hour talking to children.

Children.

This time last year, almost to the day, he and Marshal Tyrell Ridge had hunted down and captured Cherokee Bob and Ned Salter in Utah, after a long and bloody shoot-out.

And today he had been the guest speaker in a classroom. Of children.

He slid his hat on and shook his head. The worst part was he was kind of ... glad about it.

---

*A*my stared into the fire, her mind still in the classroom with Dent rather than here at home, the dozen or so book reports in her lap. She smiled, recalling the way he'd drawn the children in with his stories, their faces alight with excitement, his alight with humor.

Her thoughts drifted to the way his dark hair curled a little right behind his ears, and turned up at his collar. And she wondered how he'd gotten a tiny scar, slightly below and to the left of his bottom lip.

A knock on her door nearly jolted her out of the rocking chair. She sprang to her feet, and the book reports scattered at her feet.

"Miss Tate, I mean Amy, it's me, Dent."

Her heart lunged to a wild speed, not out of fear, now, but excitement. "Just a moment." She bit her lips to add a little color to them, assumed her cheeks were pink enough, and hurried to the door. A swirl of little snowflakes followed him inside. "Oh, it's snowing? It's only October."

"Flurries," he said, pulling off his gloves. "Probably won't stick."

"Can I get you some coffee? I have some on the stove."

"Yes ma'am, I sure could do with a cup."

"Please make yourself at home."

He peeled out of his coat and laid it across the back of a chair while Amy poured two cups.

"Say, what happened here? Everything all right?" He walked over to the mess she'd left of the book reports.

"That's nothing. I was grading them by the fire. Your knock startled me."

"Oh, I'm sorry." He immediately bent down and gathered up the papers. When he stood again, she was holding his coffee. They traded items, and she walked the papers over to her kitchen table. From behind her, he said haltingly, "We … missed you at supper tonight."

Amy couldn't stop a silly grin. She picked up her own coffee and joined him by the fire. "Sometimes teachers have homework too." She let her eyes travel from his square jaw, covered in a little razor stubble, to his hat. He realized his mistake, snatched it off, and let her take it from him. She hung it on the hook at the door and kept her back to him for a moment. "So, what brings you by this evening?"

"Well, I guess you could say I've gotten into such a habit of walking you home, I felt like I ought to check on you."

She turned slowly and assessed him over the top of her glasses. "Ought to?" she dead-panned. "That's very commendable." But it wasn't. She didn't want to be a burden.

She wanted him to *want* to come by, and not in the peace-officer sense.

He chuckled and scratched his nose.

"Did I say something funny?"

"No." He grinned sideways, a most adorable smile that made Amy's breath catch in her chest. "You just have this way of eyin' me sometimes, over the top of your spectacles. Like you approve of me ... and you don't, at the same time."

She didn't know what to say to that, so she ambled over to the kitchen table and set down her cup.

"It's downright ... endearing." He quickly took a sip of his coffee, but watched her over the top of cup.

The compliment flowed over Amy like warm butter, and she wanted to melt with it. "Thank you," she whispered, though she hadn't meant to, but her voice failed her.

"Well, I guess," he gulped one more sip, "I'll be going now."

"You just got here."

He walked up to her, leaned in, and set his cup down on the table behind her, but then he didn't pull back. He searched her face earnestly, his dark eyes sparkling with ... desire? He towered over her, but she wasn't afraid. She was never afraid with him.

"I should definitely be going." But he didn't move. The huskiness in his voice raised goosebumps on her arms. He picked up a strand of her hair, working it gently between his fingers. Amy realized she was breathing fast. So was he. He swallowed. "Are you afraid of me?"

She couldn't find her voice at all and shook her head.

"I thought when I took you to dinner the other night, I might get you out of my system. Instead ..."

"Instead?"

"Instead, I wake up every morning lookin' forward to dinner with Doc and Susan ... and you."

Amy felt faint. His gaze bored into her, held her completely still, except for her racing heart.

"This isn't part of my plan, Amy."

He started lowering his head to hers and she closed her eyes. She felt his breath and tilted her head up more. Then his lips touched hers. Pressed harder. His hand went to her cheek and they deepened the kiss. Lightning shot through Amy, and suddenly she was in Dent's arms, and his mouth possessed hers. He drank her in, long, slow, hypnotically, and then pulled away. "Oh, dang," he whispered, pressing his forehead to hers.

She should have laughed, but something similar and nonsensical rolled around in her brain. *Oh, my goodness ...*

He slid his hands to her waist and, after a moment, pulled back a little, caressing her ribs with his thumbs. "Gah, you're just a little bitty thing." He shook his head and stepped away, his brow creased, as if she were some strange, unidentified creature. He shook his head again, and grabbed his coat. "Miss Tate ... I, uh ... I mean, Amy ..." He sucked on his cheek, thinking.

"For a man who's been shot three times and stabbed five, slept too often on the ground, in the cold, and nearly starved to death once, you do seem to lose your confidence around women."

He shrugged into his coat and sighed. "Nope. Just around you."

Amy blinked, taken aback by his sudden directness. Those butterflies took flight again, wild and out of control.

"I like you, Amy."

She was smart enough to know for a man like Dent, he was speaking volumes, but she wouldn't read more into the simple declaration than there might be. They could take this one breath, one step, one day at a time. "I like you, too, Dent."

"But I have to figure this out."

"I understand." And she did. Amy was a fork in the road. She wasn't part of his plan. But she wanted to be.

He grinned, and nodded firmly, like he'd come to a conclusion. "All right then."

CHAPTER 22

*L*ike a good lackey, Dent showed up in the hotel promptly at seven in the morning. He surveyed the lobby, noting nearly every horizontal surface was covered in velvet. Too fancy for his taste. He didn't see any folks milling around, though, so he walked up to the clerk, a stooped, balding old man who was stuffing mail into a wall of boxes.

"Excuse me."

The gentleman swung around, and immediately recognition lit his face. "Dent Hernandez." He set the mail on the counter and reached for Dent's hand. "I heard you was in town. It's good to see ya, boy."

It took Dent a second, but, as they shook hands, he remembered the sharp, hooked nose and receding hairline. "Mr. Kilkenny? It's been so long, I 'bout forgot what you looked like."

"Yeah," the old-man grinned sheepishly, and showed some missing teeth. "I've aged some. I reckon you haven't seen me since I bought your pa's spread."

Whatever good-natured mood Dent thought he had

going dissipated like smoke. "About that. How'd you come to sell it to Coker? I thought you were rarin' to go and start your own ranch."

The old man shrugged and flinched, like he'd sucked on a sour lemon. "Turned out I ain't much of a rancher. All that hard work. Constant, too. It never stopped. I got plumb wore out mending fences, chasing cows. Stupid critters, they don't stay where you put 'em."

"I have been told you need good fences when you run cattle." Dent pushed his hat back a little, thinking. "So what's Coker doing with the place?"

"Nothin', that I know of."

Why would Coker buy the ranch, and then just let it sit there? He sure wasn't the kind of man to put money out and not expect a fair amount in return. But he'd already had the property, what, six years? Dent was missing something here, and it frustrated him. "Well, anyhow, I'm here to meet some gents from the Central Pacific. You seen 'em?"

"Sure. They're in the dining room having breakfast."

Dent slapped the counter. "All right then. Good to talk to you, Kilkenny."

Dent had never seen railroad men in anything other than suits. The two young men enjoying a hearty breakfast were dressed more like miners. And he noticed right away, sitting in the corner, two packs with small shovels tied to them.

"Gentlemen, you with the railroad? I'm Sheriff Hernandez."

One young man with dark hair and a bushy mustache immediately wiped his mouth and stood to shake hands. "Yes, I'm Harry Lambert, and this is Quitman Thaney."

Thaney, clean-shaven, but also young, both men being in their late twenties, nodded at Dent. He did not stand, disinclined apparently to leave his breakfast.

"Mayor Coker said you'd be guiding us out to Gilmer Crossroads?" Lambert asked.

"I suppose so."

"Very good, very good." The man clapped his hands in a somewhat dainty fashion, that didn't fit with the tough, canvas breeches or flannel shirt he was wearing. "We'll be with you shortly, then, Sheriff." He shot a questioning glance at Thaney, who shoveled one last bite of eggs into his mouth.

"I'm ready." He wiped his mouth and stood, unfolding a surprisingly tall, spindly frame from the chair. He stood almost eye-to-eye with Dent. "You have our horses, or do we need to get some from the livery?"

"I've horses and a pack mule. Canteens full of water and three days worth of food."

"Wonderful, Sheriff, thank you," Lambert practically sang. "Let's be on our way then." He marched over to his bag in the corner.

Thaney leaned in a little closer to Dent and spoke out of the side of his mouth. "Yeah, he's a fancy pants. Rich parents and all, but he's one of the smartest men I know. He'll grow on you."

Somehow, Dent doubted that.

Initially, the men had told Dent they wanted to start at Gilmer Crossroads, but, when the trio rode past a particularly odd-shaped rock formation, Lambert cried out with delight. "Look at that, Thaney."

The two men dismounted and started jabbering excitedly, picking up rocks, pointing at the rolling, sage-covered hills, and studying the scattered rock atolls surrounding them. Dent couldn't make any sense of what they were saying. He caught a few words, like anticline, tertiary, and stratographic something-or-other. For all he understood, they could have been speaking Greek.

Bored, he hooked a leg around his saddle horn, and watched as the men pulled small hammers from their packs and went to tapping and whacking on random rocks. Drumming his fingers and wondering if he was going to be stuck like this all day, he saw the edge of a map sticking out of Thaney's saddlebag. The man had studied it intently as they trudged out to this section of Fremont County. Dent didn't need the map to tell him where they were. A half-mile due West would bring them to his pa's spread, now owned by Mayor Coker. Ben's place, *his* spread, was straight ahead, and Gilmer Crossroads was north-east another half-mile. He didn't think their present location was an accident, after all. It would make sense for the mayor to acquire Ben's ranch. The more land he had, the more land he could sell right-of-ways to the Union Pacific, if the tracks went across his property.

But what did hammering on rocks have to do with laying track?

Dent had seen railroads come in before. These men had no surveying equipment with them at all. Maybe eight years as a lawman had made him too suspicious of everyone, including the innocent ... but he didn't think so. He leaned forward and rested an elbow on his knee. "You boys are, what, trying to pick a route or ...?" he trailed off, offering them the chance to explain.

He didn't miss the quick glance Thaney shot at Lambert before he answered. "Well, specifically, we have to determine the best possible areas in which to *search* for a route for the spur line. Stable soil, drainage, inclines, topographical features, things like that help us winnow down to more specific areas."

"Sheriff," Lambert stepped forward, "this is a painfully boring process and we'll be wandering around for a few days. We don't expect you to stay. Our apologies if Mayor Coker gave you that impression. We'll be fine on our own."

"We do have a map," Thaney added, "and we are adept at reading it."

"Uhhmm. I see." Truthfully, the mayor *had* said get them out to Gilmer then leave. Dent didn't figure a half-mile made much difference. Besides, he needed to pack his saddlebag for a trip to Cheyenne. "All right, then, stay warm."

Dent tugged on Ginger and pointed her back to town. One thing was certain: if Coker thought he could get his greedy, manicured hands on Ben's ranch, he had a rude awakening coming.

CHAPTER 23

A single snowflake landed on Dent's glove-covered hand as he tugged on the noose hooked securely around the 193-lb. bag of sand. For some reason, the flake captured his attention, and he took an instant to admire its miraculous intricacies before crossing the scaffold to the gallows lever. He supposed it didn't matter what the weather was like when he hung a man, but this cold, gray day with roiling clouds and a wind mean enough to slice a man in two seemed unnecessarily cruel. He jerked the handle, the floor fell open, and the burlap bag plunged violently to the end of the rope.

Down below, two deputies stopped the bag's erratic swinging and wrestled it free from the noose.

Dent was hanging Earl Flagg today; tried and found guilty of killing his wife for philandering. Normally, hanging a criminal didn't bother Dent. Violent, despicable men, men who had been convicted of murder or rape, took the gallows walk. They deserved to swing. But Earl was different. He'd never hurt anyone until the day he came home and found his wife fooling around with a farmhand. A scuffle had ensued and Earl had brained the louse with a posthole digger. Dent wasn't excusing the murder, but it seemed to him hanging should be reserved for the career criminals or particularly heinous crimes.

Or maybe he was just getting tired of dealing death.

He pinched the bridge of his nose and wondered what was the matter with him?

Specializing in dying is no way to live.

"Dent, you all right?" the deputy called up from beneath him.

"Yep, everything's fine." He pulled the rope back up through the trap door. "Tell the judge I'm ready."

Several minutes later, a group of deputies marched out of the courthouse, Earl Flagg in the middle of them. Heavy-built, head down, shoulders bent, he and his escort cut through a meager crowd of spectators and ascended the steps. Dent took Flagg by the shoulder and positioned him over the trap door, assessed the position, then moved him over another inch.

"You Hernandez, the one they say ain't never botched a hanging?"

Dent didn't acknowledge Flagg. Instead, he slapped a leather belt around the man's thighs.

"I seen a botched hanging once," Flagg continued, his voice strong but shaky. "It was a terrible sight to behold. That man's neck musta stretched two feet if it was an inch."

Dent buckled the belt and stood up. Earl Flagg was a short, heavy man, with a blubbery neck. Fat there could be a problem if Dent had made even the smallest mistake in his calculations. The knot could slip. But it wouldn't. "You'll go quick. You got my word on it."

Flagg's gray eyes filled with tears, and he swallowed. "Thank you. I deserve what I'm gettin'. I'm just scared of sufferin'. I'm sorry for what I did, truly sorry, and I asked God to forgive me. Reckon He's the only judge who matters now."

"I reckon," Dent muttered, stepping away. He motioned for the jailer to finish the ceremonial steps.

"Any last words?" the jailer asked.

Earl Flagg thought about it for a moment then whispered simply, "No."

The deputy nodded and draped a thick, black hood over Flint's head. Then Dent stepped in and dropped the noose on him. Carefully, skillfully, he felt for Flint's spine and twisted the rope two inches to the left, tucking the bulk of the knot beneath the man's ear. "Don't move," he said softly, "and the snap will be clean."

Dent pushed through the deputies, the chaplain, a judge, and a reporter with a pad and pencil, and grabbed hold of the lever. He shifted so he could see Flagg and the trap door.

The judge and the chaplain said their piece. Dent uncharacteristically made one last check of the knot's position then returned to the lever. The judge nodded at him, and Dent snatched the handle back with a determined jerk.

The trapdoor fell away and Flagg slipped into the Great Beyond.

A perfect execution.

As Dent had known it would be.

The men on the platform filed toward the stairs, and slapped Dent on the shoulder with robust congratulations. Most men reacted that way, a few ladies, too, but most women recoiled when they learned of his profession. As if being near him was like standing next to the Angel of Death.

On which side would Amy come down? Eventually, he'd have to give her the chance to choose. He wasn't anticipating the moment with any eagerness.

*D*ent stared at the knife in his hand, long, sharp, dangerous. He'd caught one just like this in the left shoulder blade a couple of years back. Suddenly the band started playing, jolting him back to the bright lanterns and bustling crowd of townsfolk at the fall festival.

Amy touched his arm. "Are you sure you want to do this? I believe Mr. McGyver would take your place, if you'd rather not."

Dent glanced across the table at Coker, who had his knife poised eagerly above a large, round pumpkin.

He smirked at Dent. "This should be easy for you, Sheriff. The pumpkin's not going to try to resist arrest."

The gathering crowd roared with laughter. Dent's jaw clenched. Not only could he do this, but he wanted to do this. And not just because Coker thought participating in something as frivolous as pumpkin carving was a punishment. He came back to Amy and gave her a wry smile. He wanted to do this for her. With her.

Shoot, maybe this would put her in the mind for another kiss. He could still taste that last one, and the recollection quickened his pulse. He could use another one now to erase the memory of Flagg's hanging ... or at least dim it for a while. "What are the rules again?"

A smile lit her face and she let out a long, slow breath. "We have to clean it and then carve a face. The face must contain at least two eyes, a nose and a mouth. First team finished wins."

"All right," Doc pulled his pocket watch from his vest and surveyed the four teams of two people surrounding the long, plank table. "Get ready." The crowd pressed in. "You'll have exactly fifteen minutes on my start." He waited a moment, raised a finger then shouted, "Go!"

Amidst cheers and jeers, the teams commenced to cutting. Dent sawed the top off his and Amy's pumpkin, set it aside, then the two of them picked up their wooden spoons and started scooping. Within minutes, a messy, stringy, pile of pumpkin guts created a line down the center of the table.

"Can you believe you're doing this?" she asked, laughing as she tossed a handful of orange muck to the table.

He grinned at the sound of her having so much fun. "No." He dug his spoon into the fleshy innards, scraped in a circle, and hauled out some pumpkin guts.

"Are you sorry?"

He paused for an instant. "No." And they laughed again.

Now, their hands covered in sticky, fibrous pumpkin strings, they assessed the flat surface of where a face should be. "I'll show you a trick I learned from a book." She picked up the ice pick he'd noticed on the table and started drawing. Nothing too intricate, but he realized pretty quickly she was drawing a pine tree with a simple face inside part of it. "The town is named Evergreen, after all." Finishing a few more details, she pulled her hand away. "Get to carving, Sheriff."

Funny how a man's mind will work over a problem while he's got his attention focused someplace else. Dent, fairly skilled with a knife, stabbed and carved and cut ... and all of a sudden he knew why Tom Packett's house appeared different.

"It's his yard."

Amy tilted her head, puzzled. "What?"

He pulled the knife from the pumpkin and straightened up. "The other day, when we were at Packett's, I noticed something was different. It was his yard. When I stopped by on my way to Cheyenne, everything was a mess. Ramshackle. Weedy. Especially the yard. Overgrown." His voice rose with excitement. "The other day, when you and I were there, the whole yard had been eaten down."

"I still don't see—"

"Horses. Several horses had been milling around in his yard."

Amy's brow showed consternation, and Dent supposed he wasn't making much sense. "Packett had to get that money from somewhere. He doesn't strike me as the kind of man with rich relatives. He's in a gang. And they've been there, to the Packett place, recently."

"They're robbing the bank!" a man bellowed.

"Stay here." Dent didn't know who yelled, or from where the voice came. Women screamed, men gasped, and he bolted, gun drawn, in the direction of the bank. The JHK Lumber Company's warehouse, hosting the fall festival, was one street over from Main. Dent cut down a dark alley, and emerged beside the bakery, directly across the street from the bank. A full moon lost in the clouds cast only the slightest light, but enough that he could make out shadows milling in front of the building, and hear the disgruntled grumbling from the horses. A stampede of footsteps came up behind him. Before he could wave everyone to a stop, the bandits started firing.

"Get down!" Dent yelled over the thunder of guns as he threw himself up against the bakery's wall. He peeked around the corner, and fired into the group of men now mounting their horses and shooting in every direction. The fire from their guns lit up the night.

Coker dove to the ground in front of Dent. Using a barrel for cover, he fired at the men. "They're getting away!"

Dent and Coker continued firing as the outlaws spurred their horses. One mount reared, its rider flipping head-over-heels to the ground. The bandits kept up a barrage of gunfire as they thundered out of town, never even slowing down for their fallen comrade. Dent reloaded, raced into the street, firing, but the robbers were gone.

Accepting it, he rushed over to the man lying in the street.

"Who is it?" Coker asked, coming up behind him.

Dent knelt down and rolled the man over ... and his heart sank.

"Israel Packett."

CHAPTER 24

When the shooting stopped, Amy followed the rest of the crowd and several bobbing lanterns out to the street. She arrived in time to see someone hold a light up for the sheriff. He had a man by the arm and pulled the lantern closer.

Amy's hand flew to her mouth and she rushed over to Dent and his prisoner. Yes, in the amber glow, she saw the boy's face clearly. "Oh, Israel, please tell me you didn't have anything to do with this."

He kept his gaze on the ground and his mouth clamped shut.

"I'm sorry, Amy," Dent whispered as he pushed Israel past her then stopped and raised his voice to the crowd. "If you saw anything, anything at all, come by the sheriff's office as soon as you can. I'll need your statement."

"I—I think I'm shot."

Amy heard the man's voice from somewhere in front of her, but didn't know him. Doc scrambled past her, pushing through the crowd, like a bear thrashing through tall weeds. "Somebody help me get him to my office."

He grabbed the man around the shoulders as he collapsed. Two other men helped Doc lift him, and they hurried away, like some odd, injured centipede.

Amy stood there in the street, lost in her despair, heartbroken over this last choice of Israel's, a choice that would most likely have devastating consequences.

"Come on, dear," Susan draped an arm around her. "Let's get you home."

Unable to sleep, but not quite ready to walk in the dark by herself back to the sheriff's office, Amy paced the floor in her cabin until dawn. But she prayed. She prayed over Israel as if he were her own brother ... or son. *Father, somehow let this all be a mistake, that he was merely in the wrong place at the wrong time. Please ...*

When the world outside had transformed from night to day, she grabbed her coat and rushed to the sheriff's office. She found Dent standing on the boardwalk out front, rubbing his eyes.

"Can I see him?" she asked softly.

He froze then slowly lowered his hands. Dark circles shaded the area beneath his eyes. Worry creased his brow. "Somebody needs to. He's putting a noose around his own neck, Amy. He needs to tell me something, anything to help him. All he'll say is that he was holding the horses."

"I'll see what I can do."

Dent gently clutched her arm as she reached for the door. "Mr. McGyver got shot last night. He died a little while ago. If Israel doesn't talk, I'm going to have to charge him with murder."

*A*my leaned on the bars and regarded Israel with gut-wrenching grief. She felt his spirit dying right in front of her, and she prayed he would do the right thing. He sat on the cot against the far wall, gazing up at the window. His face had barely healed from the last beating, and now there was dirt smudged on his cheek and all down the side of his shirt. *From tumbling out of the saddle. Does he know he's fortunate to even be alive, what with all those bullets flying?*

"Israel, why won't you help Sheriff Hernandez?"

He slowly swung his face around to her. She saw his fear, but a ferocious determination as well. "He's my pa, Miss Tate."

Though she'd assumed Tom Packett had been involved, to hear Israel say it was a difficult blow. "Of course, I understand. But could you give the sheriff other names?"

He didn't answer, and shifted back to staring out the window.

"Israel, please … a man has died. I'm sure you didn't shoot him. You probably didn't even have a gun."

"I was just holding the horses."

"And they left you behind. You don't owe them any loyalty."

She waited, but Israel said no more. Desperation clawed at her. Why wouldn't this boy try to save himself? *Oh, God, help me to say something, anything, that will get him to value his own life.* "Please, Israel …"

He moved his face away a bit more, enough to let her know he was done.

Stunned, grieving, Amy slipped her fingers beneath her glasses and wiped away the tears. She took a moment to pull herself together, and stepped back outside. Dent was still on the boardwalk, and he turned when he heard the door. Their eyes locked and all the hopelessness in Amy burst like a dam, along with a sob.

Dent folded her into his arms and she wept against his chest. "Why is he being so stubborn?"

"Shhh." Dent hugged her tight and kissed the top of her head. "It's gonna be all right." He rested his cheek on the top of her head. "I'll figure something out."

Amy sniffled and fought the tears back. Yes, Dent would think of something. She knew he would. He could save Israel.

"Did he say anything to you? Anything at all? Any names?"

"Only ..." she straightened her glasses. "'He's my pa, Miss Tate.'" The beautiful, sacrificial offering of himself in his father's stead tore another sob from her. "He loves his father, Dent. That's not wrong."

Lovingly, gently, Dent caressed her back, running his hand slowly up and down her spine. "No, that's not wrong. But he's protecting a murderer. I'm pretty sure this gang robbed a rancher over in Ten Sleep and took his payroll. That's how Packett paid off his mortgage."

"So depositing it in the bank didn't matter," Amy finished, "because they were going to steal it back. Oh, I could strangle that father of his."

"Maybe I'll get the chance."

---

*R*ight or wrong, and no matter the cause, Dent could have stood there all day with Amy in his arms. Never had holding a woman made him feel so ... peaceful. Like he'd come home. He hated she was in agony, and would do anything to fix that, but she had fallen into his arms in her pain. She made him feel connected again to the world around him. For so long, he'd felt like a ghost, an avenging angel, floating through life, dealing out death, ignoring life, intent on his eventual revenge.

He rested his cheek on her hair. As soft as rabbit fur, the amazing mix of colors reminded him of chocolate, caramel, and new copper pennies. He let himself get lost in the perfection of how she felt pressed against him. She fit him, molded to him, like a hand in a glove. If only she wasn't in his arms because of a tragedy.

Footsteps at the end of the walk brought his head up. Mayor Coker's scowl snatched Dent back to reality, but he didn't let Amy go.

"Am I interrupting?" Coker asked, scowling.

Amy gasped and stepped out of Dent's arms. She was embarrassed, but Dent wasn't. He returned Coker's scowl. "Israel is her favorite student. She's understandably upset."

The mayor's face softened as Amy hurriedly wiped her tears and straightened her glasses. "Then I'm sorry to bring her more bad news."

Dent stiffened. *What now?*

"With McGyver's death, you well know that the stakes on this crime have escalated. It just so happens the circuit judge will be here in two days, and there's nothing on his docket more serious than a deed dispute. He wants to start the boy's trial."

Dent's heart dropped to his stomach. "I've got to find Tom Packett. He's more guilty of McGyver's death than his boy in there. I need time to bring him in."

"I don't think you've got it."

Dent rubbed his temple, frantically trying to think. "I wired for a couple of U.S. Marshals to come help me hunt for this gang, or Packett, or whoever." He walked over to the mayor and poked him firmly in the chest. "You tell 'em to meet me at the head of Bridle Trail. Wednesday at noon."

Coker's lips tightened and he pushed Dent's hand away. "And what about the judge?"

"Delay this trial." Dent spoke through clenched teeth. "You're a politician. Talk him into it." He rounded on Amy and softened. "I'm going after that gang. I'll find Tom."

She clutched his shirt. "You can't go after them alone."

Holding her gaze, he asked, "Mayor, has this town ever raised a posse?"

The pause answered Dent's question before the mayor actually spoke, "Never needed one."

Dent touched Amy's face, wishing ... wishing for the first time since he was eighteen that he wasn't a lawman. "It's what I do. I'll be all right."

CHAPTER 25

*A*my slid the plate of fried chicken, peas, and cornbread through the cell door. Israel took the food and she touched his hand. "I'm praying for you, Israel."

Trying to hide behind a fall of chestnut hair, he ducked away toward his bed. "Thank you, ma'am."

Oh, how her heart ached for this misguided boy trying to be a brave man. "Tell me about your father, Israel."

He was about to sit down on the cot and froze. "Why?"

"Because he can't be all bad to have a son like you. And, clearly, you love him to death." She flinched at the unintentional pun. "I'm sorry."

Israel sat down, shaking his head. "It's all right. I do love my pa." He played with the green beans for a minute, his stare far away. "Pa was happy and always humming when Ma was still here. He built things, too. Furniture. He had some tools out in the barn, and was teaching me to turn spindles." He cleared his throat and blinked back some tears. "Gah, he was busy all the time, too. He sold cattle, corn, and sometimes the furniture he made."

His face sagged, heavy with sadness. "Then Ma died, and

Pa just kinda quit on life, I guess. He drank up all the money he made. I think that was what got him so angry. Then he fell in with Watson and—"

Israel bit off the sentence, but too late. Amy heard the name. "Who is Watson? Is he one of the men your father knows, from over in Rawlins?"

Israel started shoveling food into his mouth. "I'd like to eat now, Miss Tate."

Dismissed. She nodded and stepped away from the bars. At least she had a name to give Dent.

That afternoon, the mayor stopped by the schoolhouse as Amy stood in the doorway, dismissing the children. This time, she didn't have Israel to use as an excuse for occupying her time. At least, now, finally, she didn't need one. She didn't like Mayor Coker, didn't appreciate being left alone with him, but she wasn't afraid of him. God and Dent had helped quiet her fears.

Little Greta Degraffenfreidt tossed a wave at Amy and dashed from the school, her flaxen braids bouncing behind her. The mayor pulled the bowler from his head and followed Amy back inside. "Good afternoon, Mayor," she said coolly as she began collecting slates.

"Miss Tate, I've got news from the judge."

She clutched a stack of the tablets to her chest and turned to him. "Is he granting a delay?"

He ambled forward. "He said he'd take two days to interview witnesses, and then make a determination."

"You don't sound encouraged."

"I'm not, very." To his credit, Mayor Coker seemed honestly concerned about Israel's situation. "We have a town full of witnesses who saw Israel's horse get shot out from underneath him as he and the robbers were making their getaway. He's admitted to being the lookout."

"He said he was only holding the horses."

The mayor dipped his head in reproach. "And he couldn't warn the gang if he saw someone?" Amy didn't argue further and he continued, "Now a man is dead. A good man, well-liked in Evergreen. Yet, Israel still refuses to give us any names of the gang members. That will not sit well with Judge Swain."

Disconsolate, Amy sat down at a desk. *Oh, God, please help this boy come to his senses. He's got to turn his father in, give up those names.* "Thank you for letting me know."

Amy studied the paisley pattern in her dress, hoping the mayor would leave. His feet shifted and he stepped closer. "Miss Tate, I know this isn't any of my business, but ..."

"But, what?"

The mayor shoved his hands in his pockets, then rubbed his neck, finally sat at a desk across from her. "You and Dent seem to be getting pretty close."

Her back stiffened. "I don't mean to be rude, but you're right. That is none of your business."

He regarded her with pity, as if she were a naive little girl. "Miss Tate, you and I both have a responsibility to this town. Gossip can have a detrimental effect on a person's reputation, on a *teacher's* reputation. We entrust our children to you. I merely ask, in the event that if people talk, I know the truth ..." He shifted uncomfortably. "Dent's made no secret of his intention to leave Evergreen as quickly as possible. I wouldn't want you to ... get hurt, personally or professionally."

Amy rose and started slowly picking up slates again. Had she already gotten too deeply involved with Dent? Everything the mayor said was true. Appearances had to be considered. He was implying that Dent was ... insincere.

Though she couldn't be sure, Dent struck her as a man who was trying to figure out his next steps. The choices would be dictated by his priorities. She hoped chasing his father's murderer wasn't at the top of the list anymore, but he had said he loved being a lawman. Could he be happy wearing a badge in Evergreen?

"Mayor, I don't believe Dent is dallying with me, if that's what you're implying." She faced him then, her chin up. "And I would not be unhappy if I could convince him to stay in Evergreen, but I don't know if I can."

Mayor Coker's face didn't twitch a muscle, but Amy would have sworn she saw something dark and angry there, but he hid it well. He stood and gave her that same cool, insincere smile. "Well, Dent is no fool. I'm sure if anyone can convince him to stay in our little town it's you."

---

*D*ent had run out of time. His two days were up. He reined Ginger in and surveyed the great, rolling sea of sage and grass framed in the background by snow-covered mountains. If he had more time, he could find Packett and the others, but he would have to follow more trails, ask at more stage stops and roadhouses, dig up more reliable contacts.

If he had more time.

If he had more desire.

He was cold, he was tired, and Amy pervaded his thoughts. He was none too happy to admit he might be willing to try Evergreen for a while.

Might?

Tired of lying to himself, he leaned on the pommel. He thought about a different path a lot these days. He could imagine Amy, his sweet, willing wife, in his arms. He could run a small herd on Ben's spread, and work as a peace officer in this mostly peaceful town, only riding out and sleeping on the ground as an exception, not the rule. The classroom visit rose in his mind, and he smiled. Evergreen's charm, the life it represented, had grown substantially more tempting.

If Israel's trial was delayed, Dent would go back on the trail and do all he knew to do to find the boy's father. But, for the first time, the hunt didn't excite him.

He still had to meet the deputies at Bridle Trail, and he hoped to make Evergreen before midnight. Recalling old paths, he cut across Bud Sayer's place then crossed onto Ben's property. *I have to quit calling it that. Ben left it to me. It's my place now.*

He kicked Ginger to a lope and followed the fence line for a quarter mile, headed for a little creek that formed a small pond. He'd get his girl a drink then push her a little harder the rest of the way.

Another hundred yards, he came to the dribbling water and grimaced at the smell. Puzzled, he and Ginger walked along the low bank for a few feet, and then he saw it.

Black, greasy oil seeping into the water.

So stunned was he by the oil, he nearly missed the rifle lying in the grass on the other bank. Instantly, he dismounted to make himself a smaller target. Warily, he surveyed the ocean of rocks and waist-high grass. Nothing. He tied Ginger to a sage bush, crossed the creek to retrieve the rifle, and saw the blood on it ... on the ground, too.

A trail of it, dried brown. He hunkered down and followed where it led. In a hundred yards, he found the man, curled up in a tight ball on the ground, holding his bloody midsection. Dent knelt down and rolled him over.

"Aaagh," the man groaned. His dead, gray eyes flew open, and he clutched the lapel on Dent's coat with a bloody hand.

"Help me, Mister, please." Agony strangled his voice. And no wonder. Gut shot. "Oh, Lord, you gotta help me."

Dent recognized him. Casey Watson. There were half-a-dozen Wanted posters on him for his robberies. "You're shot in the stomach, Casey. Not much I can do." He peeled the thief's hand away. "You with those boys that robbed the bank in Evergreen two days ago?"

Writhing in pain, Watson nodded.

"I'm lookin' for them, Tom Packett especially. Where were they headed?"

"Promise to put me outta my misery," he labored to speak, "and I'll ... I'll tell ya."

Specializing in dyin' ...

He cupped his fist over his mouth, rested his elbow on his knee. The man was dying anyway. Probably wouldn't even make it into town for Doc to put him down with morphine. He didn't owe Casey the courtesy of a bullet, but the man was only a thief. He'd never so much as butted a bystander with his revolver. "Tell me and I'll do it."

Sweat poured off the man as he writhed and dug his heels into the dirt. "Hole-in-the-Wall ... but it's a ploy. They're really headed to Arizona."

"And the boy, Israel. Was he there of his own accord?"

Casey rolled his head back and forth and grunted. "No. His pa threatened to hurt the schoolteacher," a shriek tore loose from him then he curled up like a possum, panting hard.

"Go on."

"He—he said he had to come or else. Oh, gaaah ..."

"Did he have a gun?"

Casey wagged his head. "I don't know, I don't know, now, please, God—please kill me!"

"How'd you get into the safe? It wasn't blown?"

"Bank teller ... left the combination ... in a ... brick beneath the bank."

"Which teller?"

Casey writhed; sweat poured form him. "I don't know!" he screamed.

Dent rose and hurried back to his horse, shoving Casey's rifle in between the saddle and blanket. He dug around in his saddlebag for a note pad and a pencil, scribbled a confession, and jogged it back to Casey. "Here, sign this."

Whimpering now, the pain was so excruciating, Casey didn't question. Dent laid the paper on the ground and the outlaw scribbled his name, leaving a bloody print on it. Soul weary from this unending dance with death, Dent stood and pulled his .44.

He aimed it as Casey, who suddenly spasmed like he'd been hit by lightning, then he relaxed, and a long, slow, final breath escaped him. His eyes glazed over, seeing nothing.

---

*D*ent pounded on the hotel room door. Muffled complaints came from the other side, but shortly, Judge Swain opened up, still positioning his glasses, white hair tossed every which way.

Dent shoved past him into the dark room. "I've got a confession here, Judge—"

"Hold on, hold on," the judge growled. "Let me see, where did I ...?" A moment later a match struck, illuminating the man's boney, stern face. He tilted the shade on his lamp and lit it. "Now, what in the Sam Hill do you want?"

Dent stepped closer, letting the light show his face. "It's me, Judge, Dent Hernandez—Sheriff Hernandez. I've got a confession that will clear Israel Packett."

"Do you now?" The judge tugged a flannel robe on over

his nightshirt and slipped his feet into a pair of sheepskin slippers. "Let me take a gander." Dent handed over the note as the old man pushed his spectacles higher on his nose. He read it and scrunched his face. "This doesn't prove anything. It just says Israel Packett was there under duress. That's the kind of thing I consider during the sentencing, if it's even true. It doesn't clear him of riding with bandits. He could have alerted the town to the robbery if he'd really wanted to. I'm going to charge him with murder, and then see what the lawyers do with that."

Hopeless and deflated, Dent sank to the bed. "Judge, that boy was trying to make a new start for himself. He was going to the schoolteacher for tutoring. He was working to get away from men like his pa."

Judge Swain sank into a chair and pulled off his spectacles. Wiping them on his nightgown, he stared at Dent. "You care what happens to the boy?"

Yes, he did. Not as much as he should perhaps, and Amy figured into his thinking right much. He didn't want to see the boy convicted. More importantly, he didn't want to see him hanged, by his hand or anyone else's. "Yes sir."

"If I give you more time, can you find some member in that gang to swear the boy didn't have a gun?"

Dent leaped to his feet. "Yes sir."

"I'll delay the trial for one month. Not a day more."

CHAPTER 26

*A*my pushed open the door to the sheriff's office, her left arm supporting a napkin-covered tray. She supposed if Dent hadn't ridden in during the night, she could eat the eggs and bacon herself and visit with Israel. She had time to do a lesson with him before school started, as well.

As she peeked into the front room, she realized Dent was there, stuffing a saddlebag. "Oh!" He was shirtless, and Amy caught a glimpse of wide shoulders, powerful arms, and a stomach she could scrub her laundry on. She quickly spoke to the ceiling as he reached for a shirt. "Good morning. I was hoping you'd be back. I brought breakfast for you and Israel."

Buttoning his shirt, he hurried across the room to take the tray. His hands covered hers and, for a moment, they held each other's gazes. She wanted to lose herself in his dark, mesmerizing eyes and the warmth of his arms. His hands jolted her and comforted her, and she longed for another kiss.

"I've been thinking about you," he said softly. A twinge in his brow told her he wanted to say more, but she knew he wouldn't. He took the tray and set it down on his desk. "Amy, I have to ride out again, and I may be gone for a bit this time." He lifted the napkin and stole a biscuit, plucking small pieces from it as he talked. "The good news is the judge delayed the trial for a month. The bad news is if I can't bring in any members of that gang ... Israel may get convicted for McGyver's murder."

"That would be a tragedy." They both jumped at the mayor's voice *again*. Amy suspected the mayor picked his timing carefully. He eyed her and Dent coldly as he stepped into the office. He pulled off his bowler and nodded at Amy, forcing a smile. "It seems I've interrupted another tender moment. But please take comfort, Miss Tate, in the fact that Israel won't suffer if he's convicted. We have the best hangman in the territory." He tagged Dent on the elbow, almost playfully. "Eh, Sheriff?"

Dent's face drained of color as it hardened like stone. "That's not something I care to discuss right now."

"Come now, Dent. Your skills with a rope can bring Miss Tate and Israel a certain amount of peace." Clearly warned off the subject, the mayor persisted and he shifted to Amy. "If the boy has to hang, Dent's the man to place the noose. He hasn't botched an execution yet." Mayor Coker snapped his fingers. "Just like that, and it's over. No strangling, no decapitations—"

"Mayor," Dent growled.

"Oh, I suppose that was rather callous of me."

And it was too late. At first, Amy hadn't followed, but now ... she singed Dent with a burning stare. "You're a hangman?"

"Amy, he's only saying these things because he wants me out of town. For good." Dent scowled at the mayor. "I know about the oil. That's why you wanted Pa's ranch, and why you want Ben's."

"Is he making it up then?" She felt nauseated, and her legs trembled.

Dent squeezed his eyes shut against the mayor's triumphant leer.

"Oh, I'm sorry." But the mayor didn't sound sorry. The condescension practically dripped from his lips. "I thought you knew, Miss Tate. He's famous. Many an outlaw has spent his last seconds on earth staring into the Sheriff's face."

Dent tossed his biscuit down, and slugged the mayor so hard, Amy heard something crack. She wasn't sure whose bone it was. Dent's fist struck as quick and clean as a lightning bolt, snapping the mayor's head back. He staggered, throwing a hand over his nose, but didn't go down.

Amy gasped, and stepped away from Dent. "What is the matter with you?"

He flexed his fingers then rubbed his knuckles. "He's playing us against each other." The mayor sort of growled and glared at Dent. He pulled a handkerchief from his pocket and pressed it to his bleeding nose.

"Is that why you hit him?" she asked. "Or were you trying to silence him?"

"I'd say our sheriff would very much like me to quit talking," Mayor Coker argued through the cloth over his face. "And you're lucky there's a lady present, Dent. I owe you one now."

"Anytime, Mayor."

"I came to tell you Judge Swain has granted a delay. And this is the thanks I get."

"We already know."

Mayor Coker's eyes bounced uneasily from Dent to Amy and back again. "Fine." He picked his hat up off the floor and left, slamming the door behind him.

Dent faced Amy. He worked his jaw back and forth for a

moment then straightened up tall. "I should have told you. I just hoped maybe you'd never need to know it."

Amy bit her lip and tried to calm her breathing. "Would you hang that boy?" Everything they had started building between them hinged on his answer. *Please, say no.* She looked at him directly. "Would you do that?"

Pain etched itself in the lines on his forehead, the way he clenched his jaw. "Amy, I ..." He ran his hand through his hair and walked back over to his saddlebag sitting in a chair.

"I've hung eighteen men," the confession sounded ripped from him, but he didn't stop. "In the process of arresting fugitives, I've killed twenty-two." He closed the flap on the bag, threw it over his shoulder and faced her. "I don't know anything el ..." His voice cracked. He swallowed, regained his composure, and started again. "I don't know anything but death."

She rushed to him and put her hands on his chest. "It doesn't have to be that way. You've got choices." Tears choked her voice. "This town ... me. You can throw off all the old things and choose a new life. But you *cannot* hang that child."

He gently clutched her arms as a storm of pain and indecision raged on his face. After a moment, his gaze drifted. His lips parted, but he bit back whatever had occurred to him.

Abruptly, he side-stepped her and marched toward the door, snatching his hat from the hook.

"Dent?"

He stopped.

"Please say you won't hang Israel, if it comes to that."

He hesitated a moment longer, then slipped silently out the door.

You can throw off all the old things and choose a new life.

Amy's words haunted Dent as he rode through the mountains, hunted in dry, red canyons, and tracked his way across the hills. Weeks passed. His time grew short, but he would not quit. If he had to lose her because he didn't know how to choose a different life, then by God, the loss would mean something. He would find Tom Packett and his cohorts, and drag them back to Evergreen. Israel would not stand trial alone.

He pulled Ginger to a stop and peered through a thin forest of blazing yellow aspens. A steep wall of rock rose to his right, and, off to his left, the trees gave way to a broad, rolling plain. His breath and tiny snowflakes swirled in the air as he listened.

Had he heard something, or was it he'd *felt* something?

A rifle shot cracked the air and bark splintered off a tree not two feet from him. Dent spurred Ginger and high-tailed it toward a boulder. He cut her in hard behind the rock, dirt and gravel flying. Gun drawn, he leaped to the ground, hunched down behind the mammoth slice of granite, and scanned the cliff's ledge.

Dent never missed when he fired because he never fired if he wasn't sure of the shot. He watched the wall, silently, patiently. After several minutes, he decided to draw them out.

Knowing she wouldn't go far, Dent quietly pulled his rifle from the scabbard, smacked Ginger in the rear, and sent her bolting. Motion at the top of the wall drew his eye. A hat and the tip of a rifle. The man would have to stand higher to take the shot. Dent aimed his rifle. A head and shoulders appeared, silhouetted against the gray sky. Dent squeezed the trigger.

The man screamed and plunged one hundred feet off the cliff. His life ended with a sickening, abrupt thud. Confident of his cover, Dent called out. "Boys, this is Sheriff Hernandez. You want to turn yourselves in or meet the same fate as your comrade there?"

No answer.

The snow picked up. Much harder and the cliff top would be shrouded from his sight. "If you know me, boys, then you know I don't care how you're sittin' the saddle when we leave here. Upright or draped over, makes no never-mind to me."

He checked his revolver, cocked the rifle, and dashed to a big, branching cottonwood at the base of the cliff. He had a plan to sneak up behind these thieves, and the clouds would help him. He climbed stealthy as a mountain lion.

Ginger milled about below, and a few times the outlaws shot at her. The first shot, he saw a man come out of cover, the second shot, the man was obscured by clouds, but Dent could find him.

With intense deliberation, he worked his way up to the top till he was directly behind one of the men who watched the ground below.

"You see anything?" the man called out.

"I can't see nothing 'cause of these dang clouds," another man answered, and he sounded as if he were only a few feet away.

Slow and easy, with the patience of Job, Dent started easing his way closer to the outlaw below him. He picked his path, moving painstakingly. Gravel started sliding and he knew he'd lost his advantage. He leaped down from the rock ... and had the jump on Tom Packett.

Dent swung the rifle up and aimed it at the man's midsection. Packett raised his hands, but only halfway. They hovered too near his gun. "You're getting off this rock with me, Packett, and I don't care if you walk or I drag your body. Now, pull your hogleg if you're so inclined."

Packett chewed on the offer for a moment then raised his hands a little higher. Dent scanned the rocks. "How many of you are there?"

"I'm not telling you anything. Stanton, I need help down here!" He bellowed. "It's Hernandez—"

Dent swung the butt of the rifle around and cold-cocked Packett. The man's eyes rolled into the back of his head and he slithered to the ground. Ready for an attack, Dent lifted the rifle to his shoulder and watched the path above him. He heard the roll and skitter of rocks, but no one appeared.

"Packet," a voice called, "did you say Hernandez?"

"Stanton Warbly? I know you. This is Dent Hernandez. Packett can't answer any questions right now. I've come for him and you, to take you back to Evergreen. Give up your guns and surrender."

Dent heard a snort and a curse, the scrubbing of gravel. He waited for the man to make up his mind. A moment later, he heard the pounding of hooves fading into the snowy afternoon.

Dent scratched his stubbly chin. There was no way he could stop Stanton from getting away. That was the drawback to leaving Ginger down below.

Davis and Thomas, the two U.S. Marshals riding with him, might catch him. They were over on Devil's Back Ridge, the only place a trail from up here could come out.

But he had Packett. Surely he would clear his son.

CHAPTER 27

Three weeks. Nearly three weeks had gone by in a daze for Amy. She stared at the roast and carrots, and sighed. Israel's trial was only eight days away. Where was Dent?

"Tomorrow, the decorating committee will get all the Christmas decorations out of stor—what's the matter, dear," Susan interrupted herself. "Dinner not to your liking?"

"No, it's not that." Amy picked up her fork. Doc was on a call this evening, and Amy had decided to take advantage of the girls-only dinner to ask her friend for some advice. "Susan, I'm thinking about leaving Evergreen."

"What?" The woman nearly dropped her fork. "Leaving? You've only been here a few months."

"I can't ..." *Love a man who would hang a child.* "I just can't stay."

Susan regarded her with a wise, all-knowing expression. "It's Dent, isn't it?"

Amy cut her roast into little pieces ... and then into even smaller pieces, thinking through her explanation. "What if he has to hang Israel? I think he'll do it. I can't love a man who would be so cavalier about death."

Susan straightened in her chair, like a mother about to give a lecture. "Israel Packett made some terrible choices, Amy, and choices have consequences. The fact is, if he'd hollered for help, or snuck away to get help while those men were in the bank, Mr. McGyver might still be here today. Instead, there's a young widow two streets over, still crying her heart out, knowing her beloved won't be with her and her boys this Christmas."

Amy pushed her plate away, her appetite long gone. "That's terrible, I agree. But Israel's a young boy who made a horrific mistake. Shouldn't he get a second chance?"

Susan laid her fork down and folded her hands. "All I know is if I was going to be hung by the neck until dead, I would *want* Dent to do the hanging."

"That's what Mayor Coker said." Amy rested her face in her hands, careful of her glasses. "And Dent said he doesn't know anything but death."

"Because that's the life he's lived these last eight years. I think he needs you, Amy. I think that's why God sent you here. To reach Dent and show him there's more to life than death."

After Dent secured Packett in the jail, he sent a telegram to Judge Swain informing him of the arrest. He did not mention that Packett so far had said nothing to exonerate his son. But Dent had felt the stumble in Tom's step as he dragged him to the cell next to Israel's. The boy was pale from lack of sun, downcast from his predicament, but he had acknowledged his father with great joy, and the two had hugged through the bars.

Surely, Tom Packett would do the right thing for Israel. But Dent wasn't sure of it.

Missing Amy so much it hurt, he ventured to her side of town. He climbed the steps to the little schoolhouse with heavy footfalls, the sound muted by the snow. From inside, he heard a bell and, within seconds, a stampede of children nearly ran him over. The door flew open and children diving into coats, swinging books, and shoving their hands into gloves flowed past Dent like a wild, debris-filled river.

He laughed as he dodged them, swatting them with his hat, then he looked up at the door. The laughter melted away. The heartbreak in Amy's eyes nailed him to the spot, and his own heart sank. She melted back inside, moving like a ghost. Flinching, Dent followed, but his legs felt as if he was slogging through wet cement.

She stood at the blackboard with her back to him, arms clasped tightly across her chest. He'd come to tell her how much he'd missed her, that she'd never left his thoughts in the weeks he'd been gone, that, because of her, he was thinking maybe he could stay in Evergreen for a while, see if this sheriff business might suit him.

He couldn't say any of it now. "You can't stand it, can you? Who and what I am." He was not surprised, but it stung nonetheless.

"I left Swanton to forget the violence done to me. Instead, I've come to a place where it is all around me. The harm you would do that boy—"

"I brought his father in. I believe Packett will testify Israel was coerced because of you—"

"Because of me?" She spun on him. "How is that?"

"Before he died, Watson said Tom Packett threatened to hurt you if Israel didn't come along to act as lookout."

She stumbled toward a desk, the color draining from her face, and Dent reached to help her. He eased her into a seat, but she didn't acknowledge his hand. Rebuffed, he quietly withdrew. She pulled off her glasses and set them in her lap, her head down. "Oh, Israel," she whispered.

"Amy, you can be a character witness for him. I suspect your testimony will go far."

She wiped tears from her cheeks and sniffled. "Yes, of course I will."

Standing there, watching her deal with all this pain and death, Dent suddenly hated himself. "You came here to heal, and all you've done is fight my demons. I'm sorry, Amy."

"Dent." Those blue eyes of hers, the deepest, most soul-piercing sapphires he'd ever seen, searched his face, and his heart. "When was the last time you were *really* a peace officer?" She gave the question a moment to sink in. "That's the man I want to love. He wears the badge to uphold the law, and cares about the people he's protecting ... all of them."

"I care about Israel."

"Then why can't you tell me you won't hang him?"

"I don't know, Amy. I ..." He stepped back, and pressed his hat against his chest. He didn't know how to separate justice and vengeance anymore. "I've never questioned ..." A verdict. Hang 'em all. Let God deal with 'em. If he questioned, he couldn't pull the lever.

After all these years, sorting his mistakes from the things he'd done right was impossible. He was a flawed man, growing cold, fading away, losing touch with life. She was destined for better things, a better man. He could give her that at least.

"I just don't know anymore," he muttered again, drifting toward the door. He hoped she'd stop him, come running to him, beg him to stay. By the time he grabbed the doorknob, though, he knew they were finished.

And the shine on Evergreen dulled considerably.

---

*A*my continued in a daze as the week ticked down. Israel's trial drew closer and closer. Her happiest moments were at school. The children brought her such joy, and reminded her that hope springs eternal. Her saddest moments were at the jail, visiting Israel, though she tried to be as optimistic about his future as possible.

Today, she had something special for him. His reading had improved so substantially that she wanted him to try something for fun. She let herself into the sheriff's office, glanced at the empty desk, tried not to think about Dent, and strode to Israel's cell. She prayed for courage and peace, and offered the young man a bright smile. "Good afternoon, Israel."

He was sitting on the cot, reading Mark Twain. He smiled at her, but his enthusiasm dwindled a bit every day. In the cell next to him, Tom Packett slept, or appeared to.

"Good afternoon, Miss Tate." He set his book aside and joined her at the bars. He'd aged in the weeks he'd spent behind these bars. Experience and disappointment lent an edgy cut to his face, adding a few years. He no longer resembled the innocent boy of fifteen. His face was gaunt and pale, and his glossy dark hair had dulled. "You heard from the sheriff?"

"He sent Doc a telegram a few days ago. I think he'll be back soon. Honestly, he sounded frustrated. He said tracking Stanton and the others is like tracking ghosts ... and he's tired."

"Yes ma'am, I understand, and I appreciate the way he's

worked so hard to—" he spoke carefully, so as not to let another name slip, she assumed, "to try to find the others."

"Israel ..." She wanted to beg him to give her the names of all the gang members, but his trial started tomorrow. She couldn't discuss it without weeping. Instead, she held up her gift. "I brought you a book with a very special poem in it. Would you read it to me? I'm quite certain you'll enjoy it."

He nodded and took the gift from her. "Casey at Bat?"

She pulled up a chair and made herself comfortable. "Go ahead."

Israel cleared his throat. "The outlook wasn't brilliant for the Mudville nine that day; the score stood four to two, with but one inning more to play ..."

With but one inning more to play. Like Casey, she thought, *we've run out of time.*

She peered through the bars at Tom Packett. Though he hadn't said a word, she sensed he was listening. Listening to his son read a poem about baseball, the only other thing in this world Israel held dear.

She leaned her head on a bar and smiled as he read about the crowd, and the first two strikes. He read the poem with enthusiasm, and she only had to correct him a few times. He did quite well, even using inflection. Then came the end.

"... And somewhere men are laughing, and somewhere children shout. But there is no joy in Mudville – mighty Casey has struck out." Israel stared at the words for a moment more then slowly shut the book. "I guess I know how they feel in Mudville."

In the adjacent cell, Tom Packett stood up, stretched, strode to the bars separating his cell from Israel's and leered at Amy. "Why are you here? If he doesn't hang, he'll be sitting in prison for years."

"Pa," Israel begged.

Packett grabbed the bars and shook greasy, dark hair out

of his face. "What good is reading about baseball gonna do him there?"

"Reading, Mr. Packett," Amy stood and lifted her chin defiantly to the man, a herculean effort, since he terrified her, "will open his cell door and take him anywhere he wishes to go. He can ride a flying carpet in Persia or paddle up the Mississippi River with Tom Sawyer."

Packett snorted and flounced his hands like a girl, extending his pinkies. "Paddle up the Mississippi River with Tom Sawyer," he mocked in a girlish voice. He pounded his chest then tried to shake the bars. "He needs to learn to fight and to kill if he wants to survive prison."

"He doesn't need to go to prison at all," she practically screamed, stomping her foot. "Why can't you do the right thing, and say you held a gun to his head and forced him to go to that robbery?"

"Because he didn't," Israel whispered.

Amy deflated and clutched the bars. "Sheriff Hernandez told me your father threatened to hurt me if you didn't help him."

"He did, but," Israel dropped his voice to a whisper, "I still coulda run. I coulda run straight to the fall festival and told Sheriff Hernandez. I didn't. I was too scared." He turned away in shame, and Amy closed her eyes against the disappointment.

Packett laughed, a low, evil rumbling in his chest. "Birds of a feather flock together. Hey, I'm a poet and don't know it." His laughter exploded.

Fighting tears, Amy glared at him. "Will you at least tell the judge Israel didn't have a gun?"

"Well, that would be the truth, missy." His laughter, empty, soulless, pierced her with its darkness. "I don't reckon it's gonna do much good, though. We flock together. We're just liable to hang together, too."

CHAPTER 28

*A*my held her skirt out of the ankle-deep snow, and approached the half-dozen men raising the Christmas tree in the town square. She gasped as the laborers, tugging and straining, used a web of ropes and pulleys to raise the enormous tree. A good thirty or so feet tall, it rose like a waking giant. A deep, vibrant, forest green, it was a perfect triangle. She smiled sadly, imagining it decorated with brightly-colored ornaments, ribbons, and bows. Christmas was a magical time. A time for miracles. She glanced back over her shoulder at the sheriff's office, and prayed for one.

"Miss Tate."

Grimacing at the mayor's voice coming from somewhere behind her, she resigned herself to a conversation, but resolved it would be brief. She turned and smiled as best she could. "Mayor."

"Isn't it lovely?" He waved grandly at the tree now being shored up by the workers. "I do enjoy Christmas. Especially in Evergreen."

"It is a beautiful tree, but I must be going—"

"Miss Tate?"

His humble, but direct, stare stopped Amy. There was no way to leave without blatant rudeness. "Yes, Mayor?"

"Do you believe a man can change?"

"By change, do you mean ...?"

"Grow up. Get wiser." He shrugged, searching for examples. "Become a better person."

"Yes, of course."

"When I first came to this town," he gave her a wry grin, "you may have heard, I was not a model citizen."

Amy surveyed the handsome, dapper man before her, manicured nails, neatly trimmed salt-and-pepper hair, tailored suit, cashmere coat. Hard to believe he was the blue ribbon troublemaker Dent had described. "Dent—Sheriff Hernandez, that is—did tell me you'd had a run-in with his father not long after you arrived in Evergreen."

"Oh, I was a handful," he chuckled and shook his head. "There was a prison cell somewhere with my name on it. That's for certain."

Curious now, Amy tilted her head.

"Sheriff Ben Hayes had more to do with my transformation than anything. Oh, we had a rocky start at the beginning, but we eventually became friends." He shoved his hands into his pockets. "At times, he was even a mentor. Ben was a wise man, and I will miss his counsel."

"Forgive me, but I don't see—"

"I tell you this, Miss Tate, only in the hopes you will evaluate me on my present, and not my past. I ..." he cleared his throat nervously, "Well, I was hoping we might become better acquainted."

"Mayor Coker, I am not in the habit of becoming better acquainted with married men."

"Married?"

"Yes, to the young lady who lives with you, who you escort to church on Sundays."

Mayor Coker laughed loudly and richly. "My, what a misunderstanding," he chuckled, and shook his head. "You aren't getting out of that cabin enough, that's clear. May Beth is my sister. And she's returned to Wisconsin to spend the holidays with our parents."

"Oh." Amy didn't know if this was good news or bad. She'd had a hard enough time avoiding the mayor.

"So, I am alone at the most joyous time of the year." He rested a hand on his heart. "And I hope you might reconsider your opinion of me, now that you realize I'm not a cad."

"Have we established that? Dent said you were trying to get him out of town because you want his property and the oil on it. Is that true?"

"Absolutely."

His frankness surprised her.

"I'm the mayor, but I'm also a businessman. Dent doesn't have the financial acumen or political resources to develop that oil. Not to mention, he hates Evergreen. If he'd *listen* to me, instead of throwing punches at me, I'd like to make him a fair offer on Ben's place. I mean, Dent's place. And, if he'd leave, I might have a chance at getting a certain pretty little schoolmarm to join me for dinner sometime. Alone."

Amy was off-balance. Perhaps she had misjudged the mayor. Regardless, the truth was she held no affection for him and she wouldn't lead him on. "I appreciate your candor, Mayor. I truly do."

"But ..."

"Well, I ..."

"I see. Dent's still in the picture."

Was he? "No ... I, well to be honest, once Israel's trial is over, I don't think I'll be staying in Evergreen."

Again, an inscrutable look passed over the mayor's face.

Almost as if he wanted to glare at her, but held it in check. He took her hand and sandwiched it in between his. "I certainly hope that proves not to be the case. Evergreen needs you, Miss Tate. And if you depart, I'm quite sure Dent won't stay."

Over the mayor's shoulder, Amy saw Dent astride his horse, watching her. How long had he been there? Their eyes met, held for a moment, and then he tapped Ginger and continued on down Main Street, his expression inscrutable and cold.

Because that's the life he's lived these last eight years. I think he needs you, Amy. I think that's why God sent you here. To reach Dent and show him there's more to life than death.

Susan's words echoed in Amy's head as she slowly let herself into the sheriff's office. Her heart beating out of her chest, she paused when she realized Dent was not in.

A little relieved *and* disappointed, she hid her gloomy mood and held up her early Christmas present for Israel. A baseball. His mouth rounded, and he sucked in an excited breath. "A baseball, Miss Tate?"

"Yes, Israel, a baseball. Your old one is fairly beaten up." She walked over and handed it to him through the bars. She prayed that Israel would not ever have to go to prison, but since that was better than hanging, she thought a little reminder of home might make incarceration a bit easier.

"So he can play in prison?" Tom Packett stepped out of the shadows and hung his arms on the cross bar between their cells.

"No," she lied, indignant. "No, I–I ..."

"It's all right, Miss Tate," Still grinning, Israel tossed the ball up in the air, over and over. "Everything is going to be all right. Don't worry about me."

His light mood perplexed her. The trial started tomorrow. Perhaps he was just glad the waiting was over. Before she could question him, the door opened and Dent stomped in, shaking off snow. He paused when he saw her, then approached Israel's cell.

"See what Miss Tate got me, Sheriff?" Israel proudly displayed the baseball, tossed it in the air, then bounced it off the back wall and caught it.

"That's nice, Israel." Dent's tone was solemn, even cold, and he didn't look at Amy again.

"I expect you to continue reading *Tom Sawyer*, Israel," she wagged her finger at the boy.

His face fell a little. "Yes ma'am."

Dent eyed Israel's cell, top to bottom, did the same with Packett's, receiving a baleful stare from the man, then marched to his desk and sat. He pulled a pencil out of the center drawer, and commenced to writing on a notepad that appeared to be half full already.

Feeling dismissed, Amy tapped the bars. "Well, Israel, I'll see you tomorrow morning at the courthouse."

He caught the ball and froze. A melancholy expression settled on his face and he wandered back to the bars. "Miss Tate, you sure are a good teacher. Nobody ever took the time with me that you did. Thank you. Yeah, Ma sure would have liked you."

"Well, when this is all over, we'll pick right up where we left off."

He smiled slightly, his lips quivering. "Yes ma'am."

On her way out, she stopped in front of Dent's desk. He peered up at her. She wanted desperately to say something, anything, to change things between them. But she didn't know what that would be. She had heard the whispers around town, children talking at school. The Packetts were in trouble.

Judge Swain was a hanging judge.

And Dent was a hangman.

When the door closed, Dent set his pencil down and stared blankly at his notes for the trial. Riding the territory this month, hunting for the last member of Packett's gang, had made him just about the most miserable he'd been in his life, second only to the first few years after his pa's murder. The fury had nearly eaten him alive.

Between fury and misery, he'd take the fury, hands down. This misery was ... like death. It stole his spirit, his will, his desire to put one foot in front of the other. He despised the morose thoughts, the loneliness, the pining for her. How had everything gotten so muddled? *All she wants is for me to be that lawman. The one who can wear the badge to uphold the law, not wield it like a sword of vengeance ... and care about the people I'm protecting.*

He slid his gaze over to Israel, who was still innocently tossing the baseball around.

Could he hang the boy? Was justice that blind?

Was he?

Dent brushed snow off his shoulders and wandered into the mostly-empty saloon. Wandered was a good word for it. He felt aimless. No matter this trial's verdict, he was being forced to take a cold, hard inventory of his life.

He didn't care for the tally.

He skirted a table of three dull-eyed men playing a low-stakes poker game and trudged up to the bar. Rip Cullum acknowledged him with a nod. "What can I get ya, Sheriff?"

"Just a beer."

Cullum poured it and slid it down the bar to him. Dent grabbed it, scouted out a quiet table in the corner, and settled into the shadows. He didn't really want the drink, and set it down.

"Sheriff, you look like somebody shot your dog."

Coker. Dent gritted his teeth as the man sat down. "You show up everywhere, don't you?"

"I was out and about, getting things ready for the Christmas play Friday night. Saw you walk in."

"Something I can do for you?" He was in no mood to bandy words with this peacock. Worse, he didn't think he had the will to punch him again.

The mayor waved a finger at Cullum. An instant later, the bartender delivered a bottle of whiskey and two glasses. "I thought we could talk about the trial." Coker poured each glass half full, slid one to Dent, and sat back with one in his hand. "Tell me, do you care what happens to that boy and his pa?"

Dent didn't touch the whiskey. "I care what happens to Israel."

Coker smiled.

Funny, how he can do that, Dent thought. *A smile that isn't really a smile at all.*

"You realize, of course, things are bleak for him," Coker said. "The defense attorney, John Posey, said he's advised the boy to throw himself on the mercy of the court, but he *has* to testify against his father. So far, he's not willing to do that. Tom Packett may well walk out of that courtroom free as a bird."

"How's that?"

"There are no witnesses who can place Tom at the robbery. If Israel won't give up any names or implicate his father, this is going to be a very short trial."

Dent tapped his fingers on the table. He hadn't considered the possibility that, if Israel didn't offer *any* kind of defense, Tom could go scot-free. "Packett. He won't let his son take the blame."

Coker poured another drink. "Posey, who of course can't tell me much, said that is exactly Tom Packett's plan."

"That lousy son of a ..." Dent faded off and grabbed the whiskey. It burned going down, didn't clear his head, didn't help him think. He set the glass down and pushed it away. If Packett wouldn't take some of the blame, then all Dent had done by bringing him back to Evergreen was deliver a witness against Israel.

"And Packett didn't have any of the bank money on him?"

"Not one red cent," Dent admitted.

"As I said, the situation is bleak, but I can help."

Coker's voice reminded Dent of the snake in the Garden of Eden. A promise of light veiled something dark.

"How?"

Coker shrugged. "Judge Swain has ... debts. I don't need to say any more. But there is a price for my help."

Ah. Always a price. "Just another crooked politician with a judge in his pocket."

"Crooked or straight, if I don't do something, you'll be hanging Israel before Christmas."

"And why does that matter to you?"

"Leverage. Sell me your ranch, and I'll save his life."

"*What?*"

"You don't, he swings. I'll guarantee it." He leaned in. "And I'll make sure you're the man who gets to do the honors."

Dent didn't know what to say. Was Coker bluffing?

"How do you think I've amassed my fortune, Sheriff

Hernandez? It's built on dirt. Other people's dirt. Their secrets. Everyone's got secrets. Even that pretty little schoolteacher."

Dent didn't think. No rational thought guided him. He launched across the table, desiring to do nothing but choke the life out of *Mayor* Ed Coker. The two men tumbled to the floor in a shower of glass and whiskey, and the punches started flying. Dent swiped a hard right hook across Coker's jaw as they scrambled to their feet, melting snow, mud, and sawdust sticking to them. Blinking, Coker shook his head and nailed Dent in the kidney, but without much force. Dent returned a vicious uppercut. It hurt Coker, and blood spilled down his chin.

Breathing like a winded mule, the mayor wiped the back of his hand across his mouth and grinned, a bloody, leering contortion of his lips. "Maybe you'd rather hear a secret about Ben?"

"I don't want to hear you say another word." Dent raised his fists. "We stop this now, or I will beat you unconscious."

"But I know who killed your father." Coker swayed, blood dribbling from his mouth to the floor. "And so did Ben."

CHAPTER 29

*D*ent's fists lowered a few inches, out of shock. "You're lying."

"Am I?" The mayor spit blood onto the floor. "Didn't you ever wonder how I came to this town with nothing, and in less than a year, owned a saloon?"

Dent's arms went soft, like dough. "Say it plain."

Coker straightened up some and lowered his fists. He fished out a bandana and wiped the blood away from his mouth. "Ben had a son. A troubled youth, in and out of jail."

"Joe?" Dent whispered.

"Joe, yes. I met him and Cherokee Bob in Denver. Joe said they wanted to see the lovely little ranching community his pa had moved to. He told us his father was Ben Hayes, a U.S. Marshal." A puzzled expression crossed the mayor's face. "I don't think he had much affection for the man. He seemed to think it was pretty funny coming here to steal horses. Anyway, as luck would have it, the night they went to do their thieving, I parted company with them. A fateful decision, as a game of poker and a pretty redhead turned out to be perfect alibis.

"Ben questioned me because I was the only stranger in town. He didn't know Joe had been here for three days, scouting out horses and cattle ... I told him. And I told him Joe carried a .44."

Dent recalled the brass casing in the tin box. And the Wanted poster. "Who is Tom Newcomb?"

Coker's brow rose slightly. "Joe's alias." He let that roll over Dent then added, "So, it's simple economics from there." He eyed the bloody rag then tossed it away. "Ben couldn't stand the idea of you finding out *his* son had killed *your* pa. He, therefore, became very *cooperative* in helping me build a new life here in our idyllic community."

Enraged, Dent moved to throw another punch, but Coker raised his hands. "Go ahead, hit me again. It won't change a thing."

Dent's fury drained away, like blood pouring from an artery. Ben had lied. All these years. "Where is Joe?"

Coker weighed his answer. "I really don't know. I never saw him again after that night, and Ben never mentioned him. I wish I could tell you he's in Denver or Dodge City, because you'd ride hell-bent for leather after him, but I honestly don't know."

Dent staggered, caught himself. The betrayal overwhelmed him.

"I guess you'll sell me that ranch now, maybe even give it to me." Coker lifted his chin, cocksure of the effect of his news.

Dent shook his head. "I don't know what I'm gonna do with it, but I'll sell it to you when hell freezes over."

The mayor's mouth fell open and Dent half-staggered, half-stormed from the saloon.

Dent stopped thinking. He couldn't open his mind to it all. Instead, he ran on pure emotion, but he couldn't identify what he was feeling. As empty as a dry well, he rode Ginger hard and fast, until they were standing in front of Ben's house.

Had he left the ranch to Dent as a form of penance, a way of asking for forgiveness?

He climbed down off Ginger, dropping her reins. He stared blankly at the log home. Eight years. Eight years he'd dug up, smoked out, tracked down, not to mention, hung every low-life Wyoming Territory could throw at him in the vain hope of someday getting the right man.

And Ben knew the truth all along.

Fury exploded in his chest like a stick of dynamite. He snatched a snow-covered rock off the ground and hurled it at the cabin, bellowing like a grizzly. Again and again, he lobbed rocks at the structure, breaking windows, tearing chunks of wood from the logs. He raged and he screamed, until, finally, in the last rays of the setting sun, he fell to his knees in the snow.

He wanted to burn it, burn it to the ground, and all these last years with it. He realized his eyes were wet. Ashamed, he blinked the moisture away. *A man who shot bad hombres and hung killers ... fighting tears, like a little girl.*

He looked up at the purple and blue sky quickly revealing a tapestry of stars, and wondered why he wanted to shake his fist at heaven. He hadn't paid any attention to God. He assumed God hadn't paid any attention to him. Or maybe He had. Maybe that was why Dent had dealt in death so often. His gift to mankind, never missing a shot, never botching a hanging.

He'd give anything if he could erase it all, start over, be the man she wanted, the kind of lawman she believed in.

Only, he had no idea how to start.

His ma had been a God-fearin' woman, and she would have told him to pray. All that she'd tried to teach him, though, had been lost in the haze of these last hard years.

"God ..." His throat tightened up, choking off his words. It felt like he'd swallowed a bandanna, and he couldn't speak. *God, I need ...* He didn't even know. Discouraged, reeling from the anger pumping through his being, he climbed to his feet. He reckoned he needed a friend, but he didn't have the courage to knock on her door.

---

*I*t had snowed another two or three inches overnight. Amy did her best to keep her skirt out of it as she hurried toward the sheriff's office. She wanted to walk beside Israel as Dent transferred the boy and his father to the courthouse. She wanted Israel to know she was in his corner. She wasn't convinced Dent wanted her there ... but she wasn't convinced he didn't. And what did she want? A man who wasn't blinded by revenge and duty.

Could he ever ... ? She didn't finish the thought. It was too much on top of the trial.

Evergreen was just beginning to stir, sluggishly because of the fresh snow. She waved at Mrs. Olsen at the dress shop, who was hanging a pretty red Christmas ensemble in the window. She passed the mercantile, where a young man was brushing snow off Christmas trees stacked up against the wall. Mrs. McGyver hadn't been in the store since her husband's death.

This whole situation was so heartbreaking, for everyone involved.

Shaking off the melancholy, Amy checked both ways for the meager traffic, and stepped into the street, headed for the sheriff's office. Halfway there, she heard a terrible commotion from inside. Something like furniture splintering, perhaps; grunts, more crashing, snapping sounds. Suddenly Dent and Tom Packett exploded through the front door in a shower of splinters, slid across the boardwalk, rolled down the steps, and landed in the snowy street.

Both men staggered to their feet and started swinging. Packett had shackles hanging from his left wrist. He swung at Dent, missed, but the open handcuff clipped him in the chin, drawing blood. Behind them, Israel raced from the sheriff's office, scanned the street, and bolted for two horses tied next door in front of the hotel. "Come on, Pa," he yelled on the run. "We lucked out. There's *two* horses."

Dent went for his gun and Tom leaped on him. They danced and spun, wrestling wildly for the revolver. A blur of hands fought and clawed for the weapon. It slipped from its holster and Amy gasped. She couldn't tell who exactly had hold of it. Vaguely aware of the danger she was in, she knew she should run and hide, but the unfolding drama froze her to the spot.

God, please protect Dent.

The long-barreled Colt disappeared between him and Tom, and, an instant, later, fired with a boom that rocked the peaceful town. Tom clutched his side, swung hard at Dent, and knocked him down. Tom whirled and ran toward Israel as blood gushed over his fingers. He reached the horse, pulled a rifle from the scabbard, and rounded on Dent. Both men fired.

Israel pulled the rifle from his horse's scabbard, backed the animal away from the hitching post, and looked back. Tom Packett, a hole in his forehead, pitched headfirst into the snow. Israel paused for an instant, grimacing, and spun his horse toward Dent. He lifted the rifle, but stopped it halfway to his shoulder. He stole a sideways glance at his father, face-down in the snow, and shook his head. A sorrowful expression said his goodbye. He jerked his horse around toward the opposite end of town and spurred his mount to a gallop. "Yah!" he bellowed at the animal, "Yah!"

Dent raised his revolver. Every muscle in Amy's body clenched. "Please, no ..." she prayed.

Israel's back grew smaller as he and his horse barreled down the street. Then Amy saw Dent's hand move to the right, just a hair. He fired, and the top of a street sign adorned in garland exploded just as Israel passed beneath it. The boy raced on toward freedom.

Dent lowered his hand.

Amy broke free of her spell and ran to him, throwing herself into his arms. "You missed," she cried, "you missed. Thank God."

He held her with one arm, lightly, as he dropped his revolver back into its holster. "I didn't miss."

The profound sadness in his voice brought her face up. "Are you going to go after him?"

Before he could answer, two bootless men exploded from the hotel, suspenders and unbuttoned shirts whipping about them. Guns drawn, they raced into the street. Positioning themselves back-to-back, they stopped, quickly surveyed the scene, and jogged over to Dent, noting Tom Packett's body on the way. U.S. Marshal badges pinned on their open shirts banged against their chests as they ran.

"What happened here, Dent?" A tall, gaunt man asked.

"Tom Packett and his son tried to escape."

The other man, just as tall, but twice as thick, surveyed the street. "Where's the boy?"

Dent laid a hand on his gun. "I missed. He got away."

Both men exchanged shocked glances.

"You mis—?" The gaunt man said. Then a *knowing* kind of expression dawned on the Marshals' faces. "Well, I don't reckon it matters too much. We got Stanton late yesterday. He signed a full confession, implicating Tom Packett, and clearing the boy of having a weapon. He also named the bank teller who handed over the combination. We haven't found him, yet, but we will. Stanton's at the doc's recovering from the arrest." The man regarded the snowy street with regret. "Sure wish that boy hadn't stolen my horse."

The other man started hopping from one foot to the other and glanced at the gathering crowd. "Better yours than mine. I'm gettin' my boots."

Dent shook the Marshals' hands. "Thanks for your help, boys."

The men didn't say anything else, but Amy saw some kind of understanding pass among them. Then they turned back to the hotel. She desperately wanted to speak, but sensed a gulf between her and Dent. He searched the crowd, and asked two men to take Packett's body down to the doctor's. The crowd surged, swallowed her, forming a barrier between her and Dent. Head down, emotions roiling, she walked away.

CHAPTER 30

Amy lolly-gagged after school, taking her time cleaning up and straightening things. But Dent didn't come by. She wrestled every moment with how she felt about him and how he felt about his job.

She couldn't love a man who would so coldly execute his job, no pun intended. And, yet, she did. And he hadn't. He'd let Israel go. She knew it.

Frustrated, she returned the dustrag to her desk and stared out over her empty classroom, the Christmas break upon them. She loved these children. She loved Evergreen. She loved Dent. And he had all but said good-bye to her.

She had prayed so earnestly that God would save him from himself. But today she had prayed that God would show her whether to stay in Evergreen or go home.

In spite of her confusion, she hoped for a moment the jingling wagon she heard outside would deliver him. Her spirits plummeted when Susan peeked in the door. "Amy, I'm ready whenever you are."

Amy leaned back on her desk. "Susan, I'm sorry, but …"

She clasped her hands in front of her. "I'd like to walk home today. I'm sorry I made you come after me."

Susan smiled warmly, stepped inside, and closed the door behind her. "You sure?"

Amy nodded. "I'd like some time to think, yes."

Susan meandered up to the front of the classroom, dragging her fingers lightly across each desk she passed. Amy could see the woman had something to say, and waited patiently.

"Amy, Dent just spent some time with us. He told us ..." Her bosom heaved with a troubled sigh, "He told us a terrible story." She sat down at a desk, barely fitting her portly proportions into it. Amy didn't laugh. Clearly, Susan needed to sit down before whatever was on her mind made her fall down. "He said Ben knew all along who killed his pa."

"What?" She couldn't believe she'd heard Susan correctly.

"He said all those years ago, Ben's son, Joe, came to town with another man to steal horses. Ben and Will stumbled across them. Ben didn't even know who he was shooting at until several days later, and after Will was dead."

Amy was stunned. "How ... how does Dent know this?"

"Mayor Coker rode into town with Joe, but parted company with him before the trouble. Last night, he and Dent got into it at the saloon, and Coker told him ... I think hoping the news would make Dent want to leave town."

"So, Ben knew ...?"

"For years."

Amy's heart broke for Dent. *All those years of lies ...* She trudged over to the desk beside Susan and sat, shaking her head in disbelief. "Dent. Is he ... does he ...?" She was too sad for him to complete the thoughts.

"No, he's not all right, and does he ... feel betrayed? Angry? Oh, yes." The fear in Susan's eyes jolted Amy. "And

I'm afraid, when he gets his wits about him, he's going to go after Coker."

She frowned. "I don't understand. Why?"

"Coker admitted to blackmailing Ben. He swore he'd tell Dent who killed his pa unless Ben made things easier for him here in town. So Ben lived with the threat for nearly a decade."

Amy flinched and dropped her head into her hands. "That is so awful. Poor Dent. All those years looking for a killer ... Coker is an abhorrent man."

"And he's liable to be a dead man, once Dent comes around."

Amy looked up, her heart suddenly racing like a wild river. "No. He's got to walk away. He has to let it go. All of it." She surged to her feet, a sudden desperation propelling her. "All of it, even if it means leaving Evergreen."

---

*A*my rushed to the sheriff's office, but it was empty. The only other place she could think to look was Doc's. She hurried over and knocked just as the door opened. "Oh, I'm sorry." She had to step out of the way for a woman with an enormous abdomen.

"I'll see you, Tuesday, Mrs. Jenkins." Doc scratched his chin. "If not sooner."

"Thank you, Doc." The woman raised a hand and waddled on her way.

He winked at Amy. "Twins."

"Yes." She shook her head in amazement and followed Doc. She trailed him as he strode toward his desk. "I'm looking for Dent. Have you seen him?"

"No, not since lunch." His brow furrowed. "You've seen Susan, so you know?"

"About Ben's son, yes."

Doc huffed loudly, shook his head, and sat down on his desk. "He's at the lowest point I've ever seen him."

"I want to find him."

"And I think you need to. If he's not in town, Amy, he must be out at the ranch. Buggy's all ready to go; I'll drive you."

He started to rise, but she threw up her hand. "No. I need to go alone."

"You're sure?"

She almost laughed. Those same words again. Truth was she wasn't sure of anything. Dent's ranch was six miles outside of town. And it was late in the afternoon.

But she could do this. Had to. For Dent and herself. "Yes, I'm sure."

The shadows cast by the hills crept longer and longer, the setting sun painting the snowy, open landscape in hues of purple and orange. Amy raced against the approaching darkness, at least, as much as she dared. She had the horse going at a steady trot, but wasn't all that skilled at driving a buggy, especially in snow.

She focused on the road, prayed for Dent, and stuffed her fears into the back of her mind. She was afraid to be alone, but not terrified anymore. Not paralyzed. What mattered now was Dent. He needed her. She hoped he knew it.

Twilight settled, and she pulled into the front yard. Ginger munched on fresh hay in the corral. He was here somewhere, but the house was dark. The shattered windows and looming darkness of the cabin tried wrapping icy tentacles around her heart. She would not panic. She would not become paralyzed by fear.

I'm stronger than that. "Dent," she called out. No answer. She tried again, louder and longer. "Dent!"

Frightened for him now, she jumped from the wagon and studied the snow. She followed tracks over to the corral. They were jumbled here, but then she discovered one set walking away ... up the hill.

He was at the graves.

Amy lifted her skirt and hurried through the snow. The closer she got, the faster she moved, till she was running, struggling, staggering over the slippery landscape to the top of the hill.

She found him, staring down at Ben's grave. And, now that she'd found him, she didn't know how to even begin healing his wounds or the gap between them.

"Eight years," he said in a lifeless voice. "Eight years he knew his son was the one who killed my pa."

Hoping the comments were an invitation, she took a deep breath, and slipped up beside him. "I'm sorry. I can't imagine how that must feel."

"All those years of huntin' men, arrestin' 'em, hangin' 'em, trying to get some justice for Pa." He shook his head. His clenched jaws and pursed lips signaled his struggle for control. "What was it all for?"

"Dent ..." She slipped her gloved hand into his, at a loss. She couldn't think of any words to help him, except for three, and she wasn't sure she had the courage to say them.

He dragged his stare away from the grave to her. "I can't ...." he struggled for the words. "I can't live in this darkness anymore."

She searched his eyes, trying to touch his tortured soul. "Then you have to forgive ... all of them."

"I don't know how."

"You let Israel go. Now let this go." She reached up and touched his cheek. "It's a choice." *Give me the words, Lord, please.* "Dent, it's Christmastime. It's the celebration of a birth, of a *life* that changed everything. *He* changes everything. He'll help you. You can walk away from all the death and start over."

He brushed her face with the back of his hand, gently caressed her cheek with his thumb. "I heard you were thinking about leaving."

Could she be so bold? Could she tell him how she felt? Could she tell him his touch, his smile, his heartbreak moved her in a way she couldn't fathom? "I ... don't want to. I thought it might be best. I thought I couldn't love you, if you hung Israel ... I didn't realize it was too late."

"Too late?"

She took a deep breath. "I am already in love with you, and nothing you do will change that."

His jaw went slack, then sadness poured over his face. "You don't mean that."

She laughed at his incomprehension as the tears pooled in her eyes. "Why else would I say it?"

"Amy," he grasped her shoulders, "I need to let all this settle in. I don't know what I think ... about anything, I'm so tangled up inside."

"I understand." *At least, I'll try to.*

He cupped her face and kissed her, tenderly at first, but then she sensed his desperation as he folded his arms around her, drew her in, kissed her hungrily, wildly. She clung to him, breathed him in, tasted his fear and his hope. After a moment, he stopped himself and rested his cheek on the top of her head. She could feel his heart pounding crazily, even through the thick coat.

He exhaled a long, heavy breath. "I've got choices to make, Amy. Give me time?"

"All that you need. I'm not going anywhere."

She stepped back and tugged at his hand. He resisted. She

tugged again and he relented. Together, arm-in-arm, they headed back down the hill in the final light of the day.

Amy, her heart full of joy, was smiling up at Dent when something slammed into her chest. She gasped as what felt like a sledgehammer knocked the air out of her lungs.

---

*D*ent saw the tiny explosion of wool and fibers from Amy's coat before he heard the rifle shot. She was gazing up at him with an expression so sweet, so serene, his knees were on the verge of buckling. But then her red coat twitched, her shoulder jerked back, wool and blood flew into the air as if by blown by an invisible mouth. Her brow furrowed in confusion, she touched the place, and pulled her gloved fingers away, shiny with blood.

"Dent?" Her face paled, and she looked ghostly in the low light. "I–I ..."

She fainted into his arms, but he was running for the buggy with her before she closed her lids all the way. He laid her in the back as gently as he could then whipped the surrey's little horse like hell was chasing them.

And maybe it was, but it would not catch her.

It didn't occur to him until they were halfway to town that the gunman could have easily taken another shot. *Why hadn't he?* The light? But all Dent cared about was saving Amy, getting her to Doc.

---

*D*ent paced like a man about to hang. He kept peering at the closed door, wondering if Doc was saving Amy ... or watching her slip away. He wanted her to live. He'd never wanted anything so badly in his life. He knew the bullet had been meant for him. He had enough enemies to fill the Great Salt Lake. Not her. All she did was give a man swimming in death a second chance at life. He couldn't lose her.

He strode to the window and stared out at the shadowy street, but saw Amy's face, her confusion and fear, the blood on her fingers. What if he never heard her voice again? His heart writhing in agony, he clutched the curtain with a death grip, and prayed.

God, please, anything. I'll do anything. Don't let her die. I never even told her I love her.

Reaching out to a God he wasn't exactly on speaking terms with ... *comforted* him some. And that puzzled him. The white hot terror of losing her, though, remained.

The door opened and Doc Woodruff stepped out, wiping his hands on a towel. Susan followed him, carrying a tray of bloody instruments.

Bloody instruments.

Amy's blood.

He rushed up to Doc. "Well?"

"The bullet hit her left clavicle, nicked it, and traveled through her coracoclavicular ligament, lodging deep in the Pectoralis Maj—"

"Doc, English," he begged through clenched teeth.

"The bullet hit her in her shoulder. She's going to be a in a sling for a bit, but she'll be all right."

The weight of the world lifted off Dent.

"Whoever shot her," Doc continued, "used a Springfield, but the distance was great enough the bullet's velocity was significantly diminished."

"Much closer, though, and Amy—" Susan cut off the thought and hurried to the sink. "But that didn't happen. Thank God."

Dent barely heard her. *The distance was great enough*

repeated in his head ... *That was a risky shot in low light and he nearly hit the mark. Nearly. Maybe that's why he didn't try again? He panicked when he shot Amy?*

"Dent?"

He came back to Doc. "Sorry, yeah, I was thinking about the shot. Has a sniper feel to it, but it was almost dark and he was too far away. Not a lot of cover out there." The color drained from Doc's face, leaving him pale as milk. Alarmed, Dent peered closer. "Doc?"

"She's asking for you. Go see her ... then we'll talk." He blinked and walked away, joining Susan at the sink. "Oh," he spoke over his shoulder, "she's pretty loopy, though. The laudanum."

Guilt consuming him, Dent hesitated for an instant then slipped in to see Amy.

---

*D*ressed only in a camisole, her auburn hair spilling around her, Amy sat propped up in the bed, a wide, white sling encasing her left arm and shoulder. Her eyes fluttered open when the door squeaked. Dent jerked his hat off and slipped into the seat beside the bed. "Amy, how do ya feel?"

Her eyelids worked independent of each other, and she offered him a dreamy smile. "I hurt some, but mostly I feel wonderful."

Dent allowed himself a little chuckle. High and tight and cute as a button. But the humor died. "I'm sorry, Amy, this is my fault. I know that shot was meant for me."

She fell asleep, or so he thought, but her head lolled in his direction and she flopped her hand out, searching for him. He took it and she squeezed his fingers. "Not your fault.

Don't think that." She drifted off, shook her head, tried to finish her thought. "Promise me something."

He leaned forward, willing to promise her the world.

"Promise me you won't kill him," her words slurred together. "No more killing. No more hanging. Promise ..."

She fell asleep in the middle of the word, leaving Dent speechless. He *had* to go after whoever had taken the shot. And there were few people in his life he wanted to kill more ...

He touched her cheek lightly with the back of his hand. Cheeks as soft as silk. Pale lips so full and tender. He could wake up every morning for the rest of his life looking at her.

All she asked was that he walk away from who he was. Letting Israel go had been one thing, maybe he could even forgive Ben, but whoever had shot her ... had it coming.

CHAPTER 31

"Goin' somewhere, Mayor?"

Mayor Coker spun at the sound of Dent's voice, cash spilling from his arms. His eyes round like full moons, he positioned himself in front of the open safe behind his desk. Hiding its contents, Dent assumed.

"What are you doing here, Sheriff?"

Dent squeezed the butt of his gun on his hip, but forced his arm to be still. He approached the mayor's desk, staying behind a tall, leather chair. "Somebody took a shot at me this evening, Mayor. But they hit Miss Tate."

"That's terrible. Is she all right?"

"Doc says she will be."

The man visibly relaxed a little. "Well, that's good to hear. Um," he licked his lips and set the wad of money on his desk. "Is there something else I can help you with?"

How many times in his life had Dent pulled his gun and fired at another human? A hundred? Of all those times, he'd been under fire. He'd never dropped an unarmed man. That was flat-out murder.

And he was capable of it. He saw Amy's shoulder jerk

back, saw the tray of bloody instruments. He could shoot the mayor. Shoot him down like a rabid dog...

Promise me you won't kill him...

But then he'd have to deal with the aftermath. The possibility of losing Amy outweighed his need for vengeance. "You're under arrest for attempted murder."

"You can't prove a thing."

"Doc said you were a sniper during the war. I see your Springfield sitting over there in the rack." Dent walked over and lifted the rifle from its supports. He sniffed the barrel. "It's been fired recently. You didn't brush your horse down, either. Sweat's dried on him. You rode him hard somewhere tonight." He returned the rifle to its place. "And it looks like you're clearing out your holdings."

Coker rapped his knuckles on the desk. "Like I said, you can't prove a thing."

"Maybe not, but I've got enough to arrest you. And, once I start asking around, I bet I'll find a witness or two who saw you ride out to my place." Dent watched the mayor's hands. The left fiddled with the stack of cash. The right one slowly crept backward. "I don't doubt, Coker, you've got a pistol in that desk drawer." He couldn't believe what he was about to say. "Don't pull it. I don't want to kill you. You're not worth what it will cost me."

That sound of death had crept into Dent's voice. Some men could hear it. Some couldn't. The mayor could. He paused, seemed to consider things, then raised hands. "I didn't get rich by being stupid. And an arrest is far from a conviction."

Snow began falling as Dent drove the buggy down Fraser Street toward the church. Crazy, swirling flakes filled the amber pools of light cast by the street lamps. Evergreen rested in the sublime peace of an early winter night. He smiled down at Amy, and she reached across her bandaged arm to touch his elbow. Relief that she'd lived swept over him for the millionth time.

As they gazed at one another, the voices of children singing drifted to them on the air. Soft, angelic, indistinct at first, but then Dent could make out the serene melody of "O Holy Night."

The church came into view, its windows glowing, warm and inviting.

He pulled up beside the other buggies and set the brake. At the entrance to the church, the pastor handed folks candles, and, one by one, lit them from his own. No one spoke. They merely nodded, and entered the sanctuary with quiet reverence.

"What's going on here tonight?" he asked softly.

"It's Christmas Eve. They're telling the story of the Child who was born to die ... for you, for me."

For some reason, his heart started hammering. He stared at the door, afraid to look at Amy, afraid he'd see a love he couldn't resist. A love that would change everything.

"Jesus is the only One who can bring life from death, Dent. And He will ... if you'll let Him."

Her words soothed him like a balm. The song, the snow, the church, Amy on his arm, it all overwhelmed him. With gratitude. So many reasons he shouldn't be here now, so many ways he could have died in the last eight years. *Amy* could have died, and yet, here she was beside him. Blessings surrounded him, but to claim them, he had to let something go.

His gift for dealing death.

And suddenly, he knew. He wanted to stay in Evergreen, put down roots. He wanted to get his arms around a pretty girl, the one beside him, and watch his child perform in this play some Christmas. He wanted to seek justice with his badge and leave the vengeance to God.

He wanted to let Christ bring life to his dead soul.

He pivoted to her and tried to speak. For a moment, he couldn't, but he fought past the knot in his throat. "I told you I was tangled up inside. I'm not anymore, Amy. I know exactly what I want." He looked around. "I want this. I want to start over ... in Evergreen. With you, if you'll have me. "

Her eyes shining, her smile trembling, she nodded.

He sighed and whispered against her lips, "I love you, Amy Tate."

"I love you, Sheriff."

EPILOGUE

*D*ent pushed through the heavy oak door to Judge Lynch's chambers, marched up to his desk, and tossed his U.S. Marshal badge down. The judge rested a hand on the star, then straightened, and looked at him. "I didn't ask for this back. I said you were suspended, not relieved of your duty."

"I can't wear it anymore." Dent sat down opposite the judge, and started bouncing his leg nervously.

Lynch laid down his pencil and leaned back in his chair. "Tell me what happened. Not the three sentences in your telegram. Tell me what happened."

Dent laced and unlaced his fingers. "I let the boy go. I could have shot him, wounded his horse, something, but I let him go."

"Why?"

"He wasn't guilty of murder but his father was going to let him hang for it."

"You're sure of this?"

"Yes."

Lynch stared at him for several moments before finally

speaking again. "Doc Woodruff told me you rode out twice trying to find those bank robbers. Roamed half the territory."

"Yes sir."

"Was that the first time it didn't have anything to do with your father?"

Dent blinked, startled by the question. All those days and nights on the trail, he'd thought only of Amy and Israel. "Yes sir," he whispered.

"Letting that boy go was a mistake. In that moment, you became judge and jury. That's not your job."

"But he couldn't get a fair—"

Lynch threw up a swollen, arthritic hand, stopping him. "It *was* a mistake. You've made plenty of them before." He leaned forward on his desk and laced his fingers together. "Do you know what the difference is this time?"

"No sir."

"This time you *know* you made a mistake ... and you *care*."

"I suppose that's true."

"We'll find Israel and I promise you, he will get a fair trial. He's a fugitive, but you said he could have shot you and he didn't. I'll see that's taken into consideration."

"Thank you, sir."

"Now, tell me about the mayor. That's no small thing arresting an elected official."

"I have reason to believe he attempted to kill me but hit Miss Amy Tate instead. He had a Springfield rifle in his possession when I arrested him and it had recently been fired. The bullet Doc pulled out of her shoulder matched it. Coker was a sniper in the army. He could have made that shot. And I have a witness who saw him heading out to my ranch. He's confessed to extortion as well, but I can't prove it ... yet."

Lynch chewed on that for several minutes, scratching his head and tousling his silver hair. "He shot the woman you love but you didn't kill him. That shows a remarkable amount of restraint for you."

Dent hung his head and twirled his hat a couple of times, aware his explanation would sound feeble. "Don't reckon it's much of a reason, but she made me promise not to. And she's been telling me about God."

Lynch raised a hand to his mouth. *Hiding a smile?*

"Sounds like she's made more progress with you in three months than I made with you in eight years."

Dent had no response. He didn't understand what Amy had done to him, much less God. Which was why he had to let the badge go. Till he figured things out. *Justice* had to matter now.

"Dent, I've always believed if you could move past letting everything be about catching your father's killer, and let it be about the pursuit of justice," the judge held up a finger, *"through the courts* ... you could be a fine lawman."

Dent bounced his heel softly on the oak floor. He *could* be a lawman. He wanted to be a lawman. "I still want justice for my father ... I mean, I *finally* want justice ... and not revenge. Either way, his murder isn't driving me anymore."

Judge Lynch seemed to think that over for a second then slowly slid the badge back to Dent. Surprised, Dent hesitated, reached for it, but closed his hand and pulled back. The judge's eyebrows peaked.

"Just how long is an interim *sheriff* supposed to serve?" Dent shot him a wry smile. "With pay?"

Judge Lynch chuckled, then let the humor erupt into full-fledged laughter, his great barrel chest moving like a continent. "The election is in September. You have some reason to hang around Evergreen that long?"

"Maybe longer." Dent rose. "There's someone I'd like you to meet." He slipped over to the door, opened it, and waved for Amy to join him. She pulled herself away from the portrait of a governor and hurried to him. Taking her hand, he led her over to the judge. "This is—"

"Miss Amy Tate, I presume," Judge Lynch said, gaining his feet. A wide grin on his wrinkled face, he reached across his desk to shake her hand. For some reason, the old man looked enormously satisfied. "I am delighted to make your acquaintance."

"And I yours." Amy dipped her head. "I've heard a great deal about you."

Still grinning, Judge took his seat again. "If I had known all it would take to settle Dent here was a pretty face, I would have found one for him a long time ago."

Dent stared down at Amy. "Beggin' your pardon, Judge, but she's a whole lot more than that."

Amy flushed bright pink and Dent squeezed her hand, desperately wishing he could kiss those adorable rosy cheeks. He still couldn't get over how she made him feel: scared of her yet desperate for her; like he could conquer the world, yet so unsure of himself.

Judge Lynch cleared his throat. "Yes. I can see that now."

"So, there's somethin' I wanted to ask you, Judge." Dent took a deep breath. "We're getting married. Would you do the honors?"

"Well, I'll be danged." The judge slapped his blotter and jumped to his feet. "You just try to stop me." He skirted his desk, moving faster than Dent had ever seen, and embraced Amy, his black robes all but swallowing the girl. "You bet I will."

He turned his bulk on Dent and gave him a huge hug as well. Both men laughed and slapped each other on the back, but quickly separated and switched to a vigorous handshake, as if the embrace had caught them both off guard. Dent sure was surprised.

"You bet I will," the judge repeated, stepping back. He

inclined his head in the direction of the badge. "And I'll hold on to that for you, in case you ever want it back." He winked at Amy. "But somehow, I think Evergreen has got itself a new, *permanent* sheriff."

If you liked *Hang Your Heart on Christmas*, **your review would be so greatly appreciated!** Authors live and die by your kind words, and I would be eternally grateful!

I truly hope this story blessed you and reminds you of the reason for the season: Christ is the giver of life, and he wants to give it to you in abundance! Holding on to hurts, insults, wrongs, and grievances only empowers those who have crossed you. Forgive them, move on, and live in the Light and freedom of Christ's love! It's the perfect time of year to start anew ...

---

*I*f you don't know Jesus, it's so easy to meet Him! Please follow this link to discover the simple steps to Salvation and a relationship with Christ. You'll never regret it. http://peacewithgod.net/

Heather Blanton

Please subscribe to my newsletter
https://www.subscribepage.com/z8i1i3_copy
to receive updates on my new releases and other fun news.
You'll also receive a FREE e-book—
A Lady in Defiance, The Lost Chapters
just for subscribing!

In the same way Jesus used parables, I try, through fiction, to illustrate a Biblical principle. Hate is a destroyer of souls. If you were to look into your enemy's eyes as he passed from this life, would you really wish Hell on him? Eternal separation from our savior? I pray you'll ponder all the ways Christ was tortured and then murdered for our sins. Yet, he forgave. I pray you'll consider following his example. And then the truth of His love will set you free.

BONUS MATERIAL

And for a special dash of Christmas spirit, please enjoy this wonderful vintage recipe:

Kisses
Young Housekeepers Friend, 1864

Beat the whites on fine fresh eggs to a stiff froth,
then mix with it fifteen spoonfuls of fine white sugar,
and five or six drops of essence of lemon.
Drop them on paper with a teaspoon, sift sugar over them
and bake them in a slow oven.

Recipe courtesy of http://www.thecompletevictorian.com/ThePantry.html

ASK ME TO MARRY YOU—PROLOGUE

"Dear God, thank You for a wonderful . . . day," Little Audra's eyes fluttered closed, but she blinked, trying to finish her prayers. She shifted on her knees and rested her head on her mattress. "Thank You for Pa taking me up to Powder River with him. Thank you for Cookie, the fastest horse alive." A yawn struck her. "Thank You for our ranch and the mountains and the wide open spaces." On the verge of dozing, Audra smiled and her little heart swelled with contentment. "Oh, I love this ranch."

Her thoughts stopped for a moment as sleep softly pulled her into its warm embrace.

I love you, Audra, whispered the Lord. *What can I give you so you'll know I'm here?*

"Please don't let that mean Mr. Fairbanks ever get our place. I heard him fussing with Pa today."

This man shall not possess your land. Your very own husband will be your protector.

Audra smiled at the promise. It reminded her of the one He'd given to Abraham. She smiled even wider as big, familiar arms slipped around her and lifted her. "Here now, little gal, you can't sleep like that."

Pa. "I love you, Pa."

"I love you, too, punk." He kissed her forehead then slipped her beneath her covers. "Sleep tight. Don't let the bed bugs bite."

Audra Drysdale threw down the empty bucket in disgust and

just stood there. The heat from the burning barn, though, wouldn't allow her to stay. The flames hissed and snarled, driving her back. Wrestling a sob into silence, she turned her back on the inferno and trudged the hundred yards or so to the house.

She'd been warned. A woman alone couldn't run a ranch. When Bobby and Dale—her last two hands—got back from town and saw this, they'd quit her, too. For three months she'd fussed, fumed, fretted, and all but begged for her men to stay. To no avail. This would be the nail in the coffin.

She plopped down on the porch step, ready to wallow in misery and self-pity . . . only, that wasn't who she was. Her pa hadn't raised a quitter.

She'd prayed so hard these last several months, *God, You promised me. You said my own husband would be my protector. You said Fairbanks would never get this place. Please . . . save my ranch. You promised . . .*

Over and over she'd prayed for Him to do something. Pa had made her believe God didn't abandon His children, and that He had only good planned for them. Which was why Jess Fairbanks was not going to get her or this place. The dirty old man had laid his groping paws on her, trying to convince her to marry him. The memory made Audra's skin crawl.

God did not intend for her to marry him. She was certain of it.

Then what? What's the plan, God?

She lifted her gaze over the flames to the inky sky. No, she wouldn't marry Fairbanks, but a man *would* solve all her problems.

Winston Drysdale's law office always smelled of something

cool, apple-mint tobacco maybe, and aged leather chairs. But her uncle's silence frustrated her. Audra drummed her fingers on the arm of the chair and waited for him to catch up.

He tapped his jaw, as if that might rattle understanding loose in his eighty-year-old brain. "Audra, I don't understand what you're asking me."

She'd too often been guilty of praying and then running out of patience, waiting for God to answer. But she really didn't think she was jumping ahead of Him this time. This plan made perfect sense—and the idea had to have come from God. "My barn burned down last night." She spoke a touch more slowly, hoping that would help. "I know Fairbanks is responsible. My last two hands are on the verge of quitting because they don't think I can protect them. I can keep my hands, even hire some back, if I produce a husband."

"*Produce* a husband?"

"And I'm sure that will make Fairbanks back off, too." Which was, perhaps, the bigger of the problems.

The grizzled old man merely blinked.

"Uncle," Audra sat up and laid her hand on his desk. "You bring wives out here for the ranch hands. I don't want to ship myself off to some man and leave my ranch. I want you to find me a man who will come here. I don't see any difference between a mail-order bride and a mail-order groom."

"Audra, dear, I do what I do because those boys can't read, and I don't want them thinking they have to settle for some gal from Kit's place. It's gratifying to be able to help them sort through the ads, read the responses. I find them nice girls to marry."

"So find me a nice husband. You're famous for your matchmaking."

"You want—no, *need*—you need a man who either has no

home or is willing to leave his home. Those are not small hurdles. Nor do they recommend him as a prize catch."

"I don't have to marry a saint. It's a marriage on paper only. He'll have his own room. I just need a sort of proxy. Me in male form. Someone to give voice to the orders but, of course, I'll be running things."

Winston scratched his gray head, sending silver spikes in every direction. "You think having a man out at your place will get your boys to stay? And Fairbanks to let this go? You know he's wanted your ranch somethin' fierce for a good long time. And then when you blossomed into such a pretty thing . . ." He trailed off, sounding uncomfortable.

"He thought he would get the best of both worlds."

Winston's brow dipped. "Yes, and he's old enough to be your pa. Turns my stomach. Foolish old fart."

Audra batted her eyelashes at her uncle. "A husband would solve my problems."

"In the short term. Maybe." His pale blue eyes drilled into her. "Then what? You're gonna be saddled with a husband who is a perfect stranger. What if you can't stand him?"

"I thought about that. I want you to write up something that says the ranch is still mine. All mine."

"That agreement wouldn't be worth the paper it's written on. You know Wyoming property laws."

"No one would know that except an attorney. A year should be enough time to hire the hands back, straighten out Fairbanks, and get the ranch in top condition again. Then my husband can *abandon* me. I'll even give him a horse and maybe some seed money."

Winston rubbed his chin and sighed. "You're like a daughter to me, Audra. You know that. I can't let just anybody into your house, callin' himself your husband. I would have to find the right man, and that could take a considerable amount of time." Absently, he picked up a letter from his desk, glanced at it, but went back to it with keen interest, narrowing his eyes. "Maybe . . ." he whispered.

Curious, Audra leaned forward. "You've got someone?"

Exasperation deepened all the lines in her uncle's face. "If you aren't the biggest load of trouble your pa ever made." He sighed loudly. "I'll let you know something when I know something."

ALSO BY HEATHER BLANTON

I *love* to hear from readers. You can **find me** several different ways:
Receive a FREE book if you subscribe to my newsletter
Find me on Facebook:
https://www.facebook.com/authorheatherblanton/?ref=hl
Please follow me at Bookbub
And there's always https://twitter.com/heatherfblanton
and https://www.pinterest.com/heatherfblanton/

I love **Skyping** with book clubs and homeschool and church groups. You can always **email me** directly
at heatherblanton@ladiesindefiance.com to set up a time! Thanks for reading! Blessings!

LOVE, LIES, & TYPEWRITERS—Book 1

A cowboy with a Purple Heart. A reporter with a broken heart. Which one is her Mr. Right?

When Lucy Daniels is rescued from a stampeding herd of cattle by war hero Dale Sumner, sparks fly, and headlines are born. Smelling an opportunity, the local newspaper decides to send the couple on a tour selling war bonds—and subscriptions. Enamored with her handsome savior, Lucy is happy to play her part ... until she realizes she may be falling in love with the wrong man.

Ace reporter and aspiring mystery writer Bryce Richard is tasked with building up Lucy and Dale's budding affair. He can't think of anything worse for a journalist than switching from hard news to pounding out romantic drivel. The task is especially hard when he wishes Lucy would look to him for her happily-ever-after.

When love and lies collide on the front page, will Lucy and Bryce have a chance to write their own fairytale ending? Or are they already yesterday's news? A heartwarming romance worthy of the Hallmark Channel, Love, Lies, & Typewriters is a funny, inspirational story of love and courage at a transformational time in America.

~Brides of Blessings Series~

HELL-BENT ON BLESSINGS—Book 3

"Though she be but little, she is fierce." Shakespeare

Left bankrupt and homeless by a worthless husband, Harriet Pullen isn't about to lay down and die. Finding a temporary home for her children, she heads to the gold rush town of Blessings, California to start life over. One carefully planned step at a time, she's going to make a home for her family, regain her financial independence, and build a new ranch--bigger and better than the one she lost. God help the man who ever gets in her way again.

Please be sure to check out the other books in the Gold Rush-era *Brides of Blessings* series. These are stories of women who weren't looking for marriage, but are instead forging through hardships to set down roots in California. The pioneer ladies here are independent, hard-working, and not so easy to romance. Likewise, the men in Blessings are from all walks of life. They have come west seeking redemption, fortunes and new beginnings. **Somehow, love always enters in...**

~Lockets & Lace Series~

LOCKET FULL OF LOVE—Book 5

Was her husband a sinner or a saint? A traitor or a spy?

For years Juliet Watts has believed her husband died saving nothing more than a cheap trinket--but the locket he risked his life for turns out to hold a mysterious key. Together, Juliet and military intelligence officer Robert Hall go on a journey of riddles and revelations. But Juliet is convinced Robert is hiding something, too. Maybe it's just his heart...

~Romance in the Rockies Series~

A LADY IN DEFIANCE—Book 1

His town. Her god. Let the battle begin.

Charles McIntyre owns everything and everyone in the lawless, godless mining town of Defiance. When three good, Christian sisters from his beloved South show up stranded, alone, and offering to open a "nice" hotel, he is intrigued enough to let them stay...especially since he sees feisty middle sister Naomi as a possible conquest. But Naomi, angry with God for widowing her, wants no part of Defiance or the saloon-owning, prostitute-keeping Mr. McIntyre. It would seem however, that God has gone to elaborate lengths to bring them together. The question is, "Why?" Does God really have a plan for each and every life?

Written with gritty, but not gratuitous, realism uncharacteristic of historical Christian fiction, A Lady in Defiance gives a nod to both Pride and Prejudice and Redeeming Love. Based on true events, it is also an ensemble piece that deftly weaves together the relationships of the three sisters and the rowdy residents of Defiance.

Book One of the best-selling Romance in the Rockies series, *A Lady in Defiance* is reminiscent of longstanding western fiction classics.

HEARTS IN DEFIANCE—Book 2

Men make mistakes. God will forgive them. Will their women?

Charles McIntyre built the lawless, godless mining town of Defiance practically with his bare hands ... and without any remorse for the lives he destroyed along the way. Then a glimpse of true love, both earthly and heavenly, changed him. The question is, how much? Naomi Miller is a beautiful, decent woman. She says she loves McIntyre, that God does, too, and the past is behind them now. But McIntyre struggles to believe he's worth saving ... worth loving. Unfortunately, the temptations in Defiance only reinforce his doubts.

Billy Page abandoned Hannah Frink when he discovered she was going to have his baby ... and now he can't live with himself. Or without her. Determined to prove his love, he leaves his family and fortune behind and journeys to Defiance. Will Hannah take Billy back or give him what he deserves for the betrayal?

Gritty and realistic, this is the story of real life and real faith in

Defiance.

A PROMISE IN DEFIANCE—Book 3

Choices have consequences. Even for the redeemed.

Reformed Saloon-Owner and Pimp...

When Charles McIntyre founded the Wild West town of Defiance, he was more than happy to rule in hell rather than serve in heaven. But things have changed. Now, he has faith, a new wife...and a ten-year-old half-breed son. Infamous madam Delilah Goodnight wants to take it all away from him. How can he protect his kingdom and his loved ones from her schemes without falling back on his past? How does he fight evil if not *with* evil?

Redeemed Gunman...

Logan Tillane carries a Bible in his hand, wears a gun on his hip, and fights for lost souls any way he can. Newly arrived in Defiance, he has trouble, though, telling saints from sinners. The challenge only worsens when Delilah flings open the doors to the scandalous Crystal Chandelier Saloon and Brothel. She and the new preacher have opposite plans for the town. One wants to save it, one wants to lead it straight to hell.

Reaping...

For Tillane and McIntyre, finding redemption was a long, hard road. God's grace has washed away their sins, but the consequences remain and God will not be mocked. For whatsoever a man soweth, that shall he also reap...and the harvest is finally at hand.

~Brides of Evergreen Series~

HANG YOUR HEART ON CHRISTMAS— Book 1

He wants justice--some say revenge. She wants peace. A deep betrayal may deny them everything.

As punishment for a botched arrest, U.S. Marshal "Dent" Hernandez is temporarily remanded to the quiet little town of Evergreen, Wyoming. Not only does his hometown hold some bad memories, but he is champing at the bit to go after vicious killers, not waste his time scolding candy thieves. And he most certainly should not be escorting the very pretty, but jittery, schoolteacher around. What is she so afraid of? Turns out, a lot of folks are keeping secrets in Evergreen.

An old-fashioned Western, Hang Your Heart on Christmas reads like an episode of Gunsmoke or Bonanza. Packed with drama, a tantalizing mystery, and a heartwarming romance, you'll come back to read this lawman's story again and again--a story you'd expect to see on the Hallmark Channel but one with a mystery worthy of Longmire.

BONUS MATERIAL-- Includes a special vintage Christmas recipe and the true story behind the fictional Dent Hernandez! A clean, cowboy western romance with action and adventure. A great read, to take on vacation with you, any time of the year!

ASK ME TO MARRY YOU— Book 2

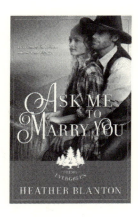

Here comes the bride...and he's not happy

Audra Drysdale grudgingly accepts that the mere presence of a husband will keep her men working on her ranch, and a greedy cattle baron under control. It seems a perfectly reasonable idea, then, to ask her uncle, who is the town attorney and a matchmaker of sorts, to find her a groom--a "proxy" who will take her orders and dish them out to the men. A marriage of convenience seems to be in order ...

Dillon Pine is in jail for a conspiracy charge, but because of certain mitigating factors, he's deemed a good risk for an unusual form of probation: serving as Audra's husband. After a year, he can abandon her and she won't tell. By then, she will have proven to the cowboys she's a competent rancher, and the cattleman next door will be looking elsewhere for a wife. But when word gets out that Dillon came to Audra via Evergreen's matchmaker, he's dubbed a "male order bride." The resulting jokes at his expense are constant and brutal. Just how much abuse can Dillon's pride stand?

When Audra discovers her father's death was no accident, she realizes her new husband is in danger, too. And she cares . . . quite a lot, it turns out. To save Dillon, she may have to let go of the one thing she's fought her whole life to keep.

A heartwarming light comedy, Ask Me to Marry You tells a story in the vein of **Love Comes Softly** and **Pride and Prejudice**. Hope, courage, and selfless sacrifices - what you'll do for the man you love. Enjoy this sweet, "clean and wholesome" mail order bride story--with a twist!

MAIL-ORDER DECEPTION—Book 3

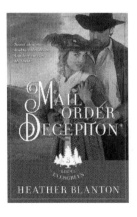

Secret identities lead to stolen hearts.

Can love survive the truth?

Intrepid reporter Ellie Blair wants a story--the one story--that will make her name bigger than Nellie Bly's. She'll do anything to get it.

Lie, masquerade as someone else ... even walk away from a man she could love.

A PROPOSAL SO MAGICAL—Book 4

Sometimes, it takes a truly strong man to surrender to love...

Evergreen's sheriff, Dent Hernandez, has to learn to live with love. Not an easy thing for a man who for years made a career of hunting down and hanging some of the worst outlaws in the territory. Can he find his romantic side and ask for Amy's hand in a truly unique, magical way?

Or will a suave, handsome ghost from her past derail Dent's plan—if he can even come up with one?

TO LOVE AND TO HONOR—Book 5

Faith. Honor. Love. Which one will he sacrifice?

Joel Chapman feels like a failure. Losing a leg in battle, he failed to fulfill his duty as a captain. According to his wife, without two good legs, he's failed as a husband and provider. Along with his self-respect, his spirit is dying a slow, painful death.

Angela Fairbanks is the daughter of a tyrant—a cattle baron known for his iron fist and cold heart. She has no doubt once he learns she is carrying an illegitimate child, he will banish her from the ranch.

Compassion and honor overtaking his good sense, Joel offers a noble lie to protect Angela and secure a home for her and the baby: one day as her husband, and then he'll "abandon" her.

Will the noble lie become simple deceit? Or is he man enough to resist his heart and keep his vows?

~Timeless Love/Time Travel~
IN TIME FOR CHRISTMAS – A NOVELLA

Charlene needs a miracle. God has one waiting ... a hundred years in the past.

Charlene needs a miracle to escape her abusive husband. Will traveling one hundred years in the past be far enough away?

In Time for Christmas is a haunting tale of love and hope set against the backdrop of turn-of-the-century Colorado. Reminiscent of *Somewhere in Time* and *The Two Worlds of Jenny Logan*, this page turner reveals how each life has a purpose and plan.

Charlene Williams is a wounded woman trapped in a dangerously violent marriage. When husband Dale discovers her innocent chats with the mailman, he flies into a jealous rage and whisks her out of town to his family's ranch--an isolated, dilapidated place no one has lived on for years. With the promise that he'll be back in a few days, he knocks Charlene unconscious and leaves.

She wakes up on the ranch--a hundred years in the past. Almost instantly she is drawn to Billy Page, Dale's great grandfather. The connection is powerful and mysterious, but should she risk falling in love ... with a ghost?

She'll learn one thing for certain: Her Heavenly Father is in control of the very fabric of time.

FOR THE LOVE OF LIBERTY

Give me liberty. Or give me death.

Frustrated writer Liberty Ridley gets the opportunity to use her ancestor's DNA to relive a memory from the time of the American Revolution. Overwhelmed by the stunning detail of the recollection, she is even more amazed to find she's attracted to Martin Hemsworth--a man long dead. The feelings must belong to Liberty's ancestor. She couldn't possibly be in love with a ghost, a mere shadow from the past. But what if she is? Frightened by the lethal fury in his own fists, Martin Hemsworth strives to live in peace and honor the king God has chosen for America. But when a mysterious woman awakens his heart, he realizes some passions a man lives for, some he dies for...and others he'll kill for. What will he do For the Love of Liberty?

This is a standalone book in the time-travel collection, Timeless Love.

GRACE BE A LADY

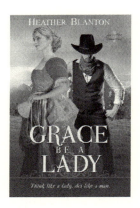

Act like a man. Think like a lady.

Banished to the dusty cow town of Misery for an alleged affair, Grace Hendrick wants nothing more than to get her son away from the clutches of his abusive father Bull, back in Chicago. But if she dares to return home, Bull has promised Grace she'll never see their son again. She has no choice but to accept her situation--temporarily. Struggling to figure a way to survive, she refuses to consider prostitution. The hamlet of Misery, however, isn't brimming over with jobs for respectable women. Fueled by hate and desperation, she concocts a shocking plan to find work.

Thad Walker is the middle son of the oldest, most successful cattle baron in Wyoming, and he always puts the ranch first. One chance meeting with Grace Hendrick, though, batters his focus like a hail storm in July. And there couldn't be a worse time to lose his focus.

A true Western saga written in the the vein of Lonesome Dove and Redeeming Love, truth weaves seamlessly with fiction in Grace be a Lady to deliver a stunning tale of love blossoming in a field of violence.

~Sweethearts of Jubilee Springs Series~

A GOOD MAN COMES AROUND—Book 8

She has a list of qualifications for her groom.

He doesn't measure up.

But sometimes, a good man comes around.

Based on a true story ... Oliver Martin is a shiftless, mischievous no-account. But he wasn't always. Jilted at the altar, he takes nothing seriously anymore and now spends his days looking for a drink or trouble, whichever comes first. John Fowler, Oliver's friend and business partner, spends his time trying to keep Oliver out of trouble. Tired of rescuing the young man, Fowler decides a wife might bring back the old, steady Oliver. He applies for a mail order bride for the lad—but secretly.

Abigail Holt spent ten years married to a belligerent drunk. Now widowed, she's worn out trying to make ends meet and raise her boys alone. She has decided to become a mail order bride—in her estimation, the perfect way to pick a husband—using pure logic and a rational mind. Marrying for love the first time resulted in a train wreck. She wants to find a good man who is qualified to raise her sons. Romantic entanglements will not be part of the bargain.

She arrives in Jubilee Springs ready to wed Oliver—who has never heard of her. Perhaps that's a Godsend as he clearly doesn't meet her standards. The mail order fiasco ends Abigail's desire to ever be a bride again, and that's just fine with Oliver. He has no intention of ever getting his heart broken again.

But love and life—and even tragedy—can't be avoided. In fact, trying to run from them may do more harm than good ...

Made in the USA
Columbia, SC
01 September 2019